The Neanderthals

A Story of Courage

Pamela Loveridge

Published in 2015
by Pamela Loveridge

Interior layout and cover design
by Publicious Pty Ltd
www.publicious.com.au

Book cover image supplied by
Mark Thiessen/National Geographic Creative

Catalogue-in-Publication details available
from the National Library of Australia

ISBN: 978-0-9925794-0-1

Also available in ebook
ebook ISBN: 978-0-9925794-1-8

To my beautiful family, Desiree, Lonneke and Chloe, and Dior, Ilona and Jemima.
I love you all so much
"The Clan is everything."

Contents

Author's Foreword

My interest in the Neanderthals was first aroused during a visit to the Dordogne region in south-west France, where I visited a museum showing some of their ancient tools and artefacts. Firstly, I was rather shocked to see the real-life reproduction of the Neanderthals, depicting individuals with fair skin and red hair, looking a lot like modern man. I had never imagined this, always thinking of the Neanderthals as looking more apish or prehistoric.

The next surprise for me came when I compared a display of their tools with a display of the tools of modern man, who lived in the same area but at a much later time, as the tools of both looked very similar to me. Again, I had always imagined the Neanderthals as being much more primitive beings, and certainly expected their tools to reflect this. I venture to say that probably most people today still think of the Neanderthals as some more primitive, brutish and less intelligent precursor of modern man, and I now feel this does them a grave injustice. After the trip to France I concluded that I really had a very poor understanding of the Neanderthals, and this stimulated an interest to find out more about them.

As stated earlier, the Neanderthals looked different from modern man who was evolving in Africa, as it was the Neanderthals who had fair skin, some with red or lighter-coloured hair, and sometimes deep-set, light-pigmented eyes. At a time when the earth was undergoing ice ages and climate changes, and some parts of Europe were covered in ice sheets, then here the fairer or less-pigmented skin of the Neanderthals was probably an adaptation. The advantage of such an adaptation being that the lighter skin colour allows the skin to manufacture more vitamin D, which is essential for bone growth.

Compared to modern man, the Neanderthals had shorter legs and were generally shorter with a stockier build. They had a much thicker and heavier skull with protruding, heavy brow ridges, and a mouth thrust forward with a smaller chin. They had a narrow, flat, receding forehead, and a broad nose.

They had a large rib cage, and very strong leg, ankle and wrist bones. They had broad hipbones and a different pelvic alignment, so their gait would not have been as graceful or as quick as modern man's. Thus we can see they were physically very powerful with their strong bones and strong musculature, and would have had great physical endurance.

Today some people still ridicule the Neanderthals' intelligence, but it should be noted that they had a large brain case similar in volume, if not slightly larger, than that of modern man. I really can't see why they should have been less intelligent than we are.

Looking at Neanderthal prehistory, we need to go right back to *Homo erectus*, who originally evolved in Africa over two million years BP (Before Present). It is known that *Homo erectus* also populated different parts of the world, with the oldest fossil that was found out of Africa dated to 1.8 million years BP in the Caucasus, about 800,000 years BP in Europe, and the most recent find being in Java, dated to 100,000 years BP.

The Neanderthal forebears are considered to be *Homo heidelbergensis*, who was known in Africa, Europe, the Middle East and possibly China between about 600,000 and 300,000 years BP. One theory is that the Neanderthal or *Homo neanderthalensis* underwent an evolutionary transition from *Homo heidelbergensis*, who in turn probably originated from the archaic human, *Homo erectus*. It is thought that modern man underwent a similar evolutionary transition from *Homo erectus* to *Homo heidelbergensis* or some other intermediary species.

There have been fossils found in the Sima caves in Northern Spain, which have a combination of *Homo heidelbergensis* and *Homo neanderthalensis* characteristics, and this shows an evolutionary transition was taking place in Europe some 400,000 years BP. In the next to last ice age, around 250,000 years BP, the development of the Neanderthals finally began. The oldest absolute dates, from stone tools found in the same layer as Neanderthal remains, show the Neanderthals lived in north-eastern France 175,000 years BP. It is believed that the Neanderthals never lived in Africa, as no Neanderthal fossils have been found there.

The main phase of Neanderthal development lies within the Upper Pleistocene period, which was from 127,000 to 27,000 BP. During this period the Neanderthals populated central Europe, central Asia and the Near East. Fossil sites, mostly in caves, have been found in Germany, France, Belgium, Italy, Gibraltar, the Czech Republic, Hungary, Croatia, the Ukraine, Uzbekistan, Israel, Kurdistan, Portugal and Syria. The best-known or "classic" Neanderthals lived from 70,000 to 39,000 years BP, and were often associated with cold-adapted animals such as reindeer and mammoth.

During the Upper Pleistocene period, the Neanderthals came into contact with modern man, *Homo sapiens*. Recent research work from Professor Thomas Higham shows an overlap of 2600 to 5400 years when the two groups both coexisted in Europe. The data from this research indicates the disappearance of the Neanderthals occurred at different times in different regions.

Recent successful DNA sequencing of fossil Neanderthal teeth has answered the long-asked question of whether or not interbreeding took place between the Neanderthals and modern man. The most recent research shows that indeed interbreeding definitely took place between the Neanderthals and modern man. This is really an interesting discovery, as in nature only like species are able to interbreed and reproduce successfully, and thus this shows that Neanderthals and modern man were similar enough to do this. The DNA sequencing of the Neanderthal genome undertaken in 2010 at the Max Planck Institute shows that Neanderthals have contributed approximately one to four per cent to the genome of non-Africans. So when did this interbreeding occur, and how often did it take place before the Neanderthals became extinct?

Firstly let us look at modern man's development. Recent genetic evidence shows that modern man seems to have originated as a single genetic group in Africa about 190,000 BP and was probably derived from a core of 2000 to 10,000 Africans. The first opportunity for interbreeding with the Neanderthals came with the first major movement of modern man out of Africa, occurring some 125,000 BP during a period of interglacial warming. At this time the grasslands spread across the Sahara and this allowed people from the south to follow game into North Africa and beyond into the Levant (an area of the eastern Mediterranean now occupied by countries such as Lebanon, Syria and Israel) where the Neanderthals were already living.

However, about 90,000 BP, there was a brief but devastating climate freeze and the Levant turned to extreme desert. Fossil records of modern man peter out at this time, and it is thought that after the climate freeze, the deserted area was again inhabited by the Neanderthals who were probably forced southwards towards the Mediterranean by glaciers advancing from the north. In his book *Out of Eden: The Peopling of the World,* Stephen Oppenheimer says the second major movement out of Africa occurred around 85,000 years BP, by a different route through the Yemen, and then through South Asia. About 50,000 years BP, a moist warm climate phase greened the Arabian Desert sufficiently to open an area known as the Fertile Crescent and so allow these people to migrate north-westwards towards the Levant and Turkey and on to Europe.

Thus the Neanderthals managed to keep a separate identity from modern man in Europe until about 40,000 to 45,000 years BP, when modern man finally entered Europe for the first time. There were two other proposed points of entry into Europe for modern man, one from Morocco across to Spain as is the case in this story, and the other from Tunisia to Italy via Sicily. However, not as much seems to be said about these two entry points, as they probably had a more minor role, because they involved a substantial water crossing for modern man to achieve.

We can only speculate on how the Neanderthals actually cohabitated with modern man. Was it a peaceful coexistence, either as separate cultures or with some intermingling and then with peaceful interbreeding? Or could there have been a more violent existence, especially as modern man's presence increasingly encroached into the Neanderthal domain? Perhaps it was a mixture of all these scenarios, making it more difficult for the Neanderthals to remain a distinct entity. Professor Higham also suggests that the Neanderthals may have survived in dwindling populations in pockets of Europe before they became extinct.

The Neanderthals were able to adapt to the harsh climates of central Europe that occurred as a result of past ice ages. Between the years 200,000 to 30,000 BP there were four great cold periods, and between these periods there were warmer spells called interglacial periods, while between 120,000 to 11,000 years BP there were as many as twenty lesser cooling and warming cycles. The Neanderthals were able to adapt to climate changes that included temperature fluctuations of up to ten degrees Celsius in average annual temperature within a decade. They were the first people who knew how to defy the cold periods of the Ice Age, and one could surmise they must have been very focused on daily survival to achieve this.

Some think the very harsh and challenging climactic conditions probably helped to keep their population numbers low. I also think they may have had a natural cultural leaning towards living in small groups, unlike modern man who is more social by nature. I like to speculate that because of their low population numbers, the Neanderthals almost by necessity probably adopted a co-operative lifestyle with one another. It certainly would have been a case of co-operate or perish in the very harsh climactic conditions over the millennium!

Also, it is just as reasonable to speculate that such a co-operative and non-aggressive disposition may have also actually been part of their genetic encoding. Certainly there is a precedent in the primate kingdom, as is the case with the bonobo, which is an exceptionally peaceful great ape that evolved in isolation in the Congo region of Africa. Thus it would not be unreasonable to wonder if the Neanderthals could have actually been a kinder and more gentle group of people, and in their own way be more civilised than many of us are today. This is the tack I have chosen to take in my story.

There seems to be little evidence of ancient rock art or religious works found with the Neanderthal fossils. However, some jewellery such as pendants and some coloured ochres have been found with their fossil remains. It is not known how they utilised the ochres, although some speculate it was used as markings on the skin. Again, compared to modern man, some of whom have left rock artworks in abundance, we are left wondering about the near absence of artworks in the caves of Neanderthal fossils.

Again, some think this could also be a result of the low numbers living in such harsh climactic conditions, where there was only time for making tools and other essential items for existence. Equally it could also be a genetic difference from modern man who has a more artistic genetic make-up, or even perhaps it is a combination of both. I tend to lean towards the genetic explanation in this matter.

We only have to look at any different culture today in our world to see that superstition and the concept of gods and religion seem to be hardwired into the brains of modern man. But this may not have been the case with the Neanderthals. One could speculate that by coming down a similar but different evolutionary pathway from modern man, it is possible they may not have had any religious leanings with concepts of gods or higher beings, and thus such thoughts may never have played a part in their daily lives. Perhaps the reason that no religious artefacts have been found with their fossils is for the simple reason that there was no religion!

It is said the Neanderthals scattered throughout Europe and the Middle East probably lived in isolated clans of fifteen to thirty people. Unlike modern man at that time, who was living in Africa in tribal villages or living a nomadic lifestyle, the Neanderthals tended to still be cave dwellers, as was the case with the more primitive and ancient peoples from whom they had evolved. However, examination of a cave dwelling in northern Italy containing extensive Neanderthal fossils shows that their daily living was quite organised, in so far as there were different areas for working and preparing food separate from sleeping areas. It appears that meals were prepared at the mouth of the cave, and sharp items were kept away from the living areas. As well, most animal bones were concentrated outside the cave shelter, thus ensuring there were no rotting bones inside the cave.

Fossils show evidence that the Neanderthals had the hyoid bone, which is essential for speech, and DNA evidence shows they had the FOXP2 gene also crucial for speech, although some experts consider their actual voices may have sounded different from ours. Because they had the ability for speech, one could envisage they certainly had speech, and also the presence of some form of structured language, which would have led to or followed on from enhanced social development. There is evidence that the Neanderthals buried their dead, and often in the caves in which they lived. They also cared for their sick and injured, as evidenced from fossil remains discovered where significant injuries had healed long before death.

It is interesting that at the time modern man first appeared in Europe, some 40,000 to 45,000 years BP, both the Neanderthals and modern man made their stone tools the same way, by what is known as the Levallois technique. This technique, which for its time was still quite sophisticated, allowed the maker of the stone tool to map out the final shape of the flake, which could then be struck off from its core with a single blow, allowing much more control over tool making. At that time, both Neanderthals and modern man made numerous but similar types of stone tools, which had various different usages. They both had a substantial toolkit!

I think that if the Neanderthals were still alive today, we would pass them in the street without a second look, as we are so closely related. In time as we come to better understand our genetic make-up, and how it has been shaped through evolution, then we shall also better understand the contribution made by all of our forebears. The latest research shows hybridisation such as with the Neanderthals, Denisovans and perhaps even with Enigma Man, and others yet undiscovered, may have played a major part in our genetic make-up. Thus the evolution of modern man may be more complicated than currently realised.

Maybe we can already recognise what I believe are some of our Neanderthal traits, such as the person who can't sing in tune, the person learning ballroom dancing who seems to have two left feet, the atheist, the workaholic, the animal conservationist, the history buff, the logistics expert or even the champion wrestler.

In my story, I present the Neanderthals with a very human persona, and I believe that the evidence uncovered so far makes this assumption a very realistic prospect. The story is set about 41,000 years ago in south-western France, just at the onset of a global cooling. However, life is not yet too harsh for the Neanderthals in my story, as there is still plenty of game around to hunt.

I sincerely believe that the Neanderthals deserve our greatest respect, due recognition and praise for their amazing feats of courage and survival. They lived in small, isolated clans, sometimes in very harsh conditions, for well over two hundred thousand years.

1

The Hunt

Silence is the killer,
Patience is the weapon.
The animals are family,
We kill only what we need.

Fasoma's question has taken Ula by surprise. Fasoma has asked, "Tell me, Ula, what has been the happiest moon of your life?"

This is not something Ula has ever thought about, yet somehow she knows the answer straight away. "It is the moon of the last hunt I had with Tula and Toma. I can remember everything as though it just happened last moon."

Now it is Fasoma's turn to be surprised. She had not expected that just an ordinary hunt could be so memorable. "Will you tell me about this hunt, Ula?"

Ula looks up at Fasoma, with almost an expression of astonishment. She had never expected anyone to ask her to share her own very private memories. Clan members rarely talk about their feelings, preferring to discuss only practical matters affecting the Clan's welfare. Besides, when does a Clan member ever have the time to spend listening to old stories told by a Clan elder, especially these moons?

After death, the Clan usually includes a dead Clan member's important deeds in their chanting ceremonies. Although Ula's deeds are so important, they are already part of the Clan's chanting history. Ula had thought that when the time came for her to die, no one would have known what had been her happiest moon. Now someone will know; Fasoma will know. Somehow the thought pleases her.

"Meta meta, Fasoma. I will try not to talk too long." Ula begins, "Of course then we were still living up at the old cave complex on top of the ridges. We had just held a Clan meeting and permission had been given to allow Tula to join the next hunt of the Great Hairy Beast. I can remember he was very excited about it.

"This was actually going to be a very dangerous hunt, because at that meeting we had also decided to try and kill two animals, instead of just one. The Clan had never tried to kill two Great Hairy Beasts at the one hunt before. This was really the reason that Tula was allowed to join the hunt, as we needed an extra male hunter. Tula had not fully reached his adulthood yet, but the Clan members still decided he could join.

"I asked permission not to be a female hunter on this hunt, as I thought it would be too risky to have the whole family involved at the same time. The Clan gave their approval for that.

"But I still really wanted my family to go on a hunt together, just the three of us, before Tula went on the hunt to kill the Great Hairy Beast. So I asked the Clan members if we could do the last hunt before the Clan left the cave complex for the hunt of the Great Hairy Beast. They agreed to that as well. So it was decided at that meeting that Toma, Tula and I would go down to the large flat rock area at the river, the next moon, and hunt the animal with soft eyes.

"In a way this was always going to be a special meal for all the Clan members too, as this animal has always been one of our favourite animals to eat. We have always loved the strong rich flavour of the meat, especially when cooked with a large lump of fat on top. So we usually saved the hunt of the animal with soft eyes for special occasions, and the last hunt before the hunt of the Great Hairy Beast seemed to be such an occasion.

"The Clan members also decided that after this last hunt with the three hunters, Toma would be the one to leave the cave complex the following moon to head out to the valley to see if the herd of the Great Hairy Beast had arrived yet. So you see, Fasoma, that moon was so special to me as it turned out to be the last hunt and last moon that Toma, Tula and I spent together.

"I remember that the three of us were happy and excited when we set off for the hunt at sunrise. It was a long walk down from the old cave complex, through the ravines and hidden passes to the large flat rock area, and it took nearly a half moon before we approached the area. We were very talkative along the way as there were so many exciting things to discuss. I remember Tula saying, 'I think you did very good work, Mada, convincing the Clan members that we needed to kill two Great Hairy Beasts this season, instead of just one. But best of all, Mada, I was very pleased that you were the one who suggested I should be allowed to join the hunt of the Great Hairy Beast.'

"In truth, Fasoma, Tula was just too young to understand the seriousness of the very matter that had led me to have the Clan members agree to kill two Great Hairy Beasts instead of just one. You see I was the first Clan member who seemed to notice the seasons were getting colder. I certainly was becoming very worried about that. However, at that moment, out on the hunt with my family, I really did not want to talk about the matter with Tula. I just wanted him to enjoy his excitement of reaching adulthood and also taking part in his first hunt of the Great Hairy Beast.

"It is hard for you to understand how important the hunt of the Great Hairy Beast really was for the Clan. At that time, when a male or female child was given permission to take part in the hunt, then this meant the Clan child was now considered to be an adult member of the Clan. And of course it meant that on reaching adulthood, then the Clan member would be expected to take on all the responsibilities of an adult. I could see that once Tula had been given the Clan's permission to go on the hunt, he was already thinking of himself as very much an adult.

"There were just so many other matters that were all part of this great hunt. For instance there was the making of the *gazzat*, something of course our Clan no longer does. And speaking of gazzats," says Ula to Fasoma, "for the last few moons before we left for our hunt down at the large flat rock area, Toma had been so very busy preparing Tula's gazzat for the hunt of the Great Hairy Beast. Only those Clan members taking part in the hunt were allowed to wear the gazzat, so it was considered to be very special. The gazzat itself was made from the hide of the Great Hairy Beast. Toma had already saved part of the hide from the animal killed at the hunt the previous full season, and had carefully put it aside, keeping it especially until it was time to make this gazzat for Tula.

"Clan members made the gazzat by taking two cuttings of the hide, with the back cutting always being longer. The two pieces were then partly sewn together at the sides, and the longer back section was then drawn up between the legs. This was held by a tie that threaded through the hide and fastened at the front of the waist. The very moon before our hunt, Toma had just finished sewing on the pockets. These were padded to offer extra protection to the male hunters for their male parts. The hunters also always wore special knee protectors on the hunt. These provided good protection for the Clan members' knees, and also helped them to grip the animals when they were on top of them.

"That moon Tula got to try on his gazzat for the first time, and was actually squealing with excitement. He was running round the cave with his new hand spear, practising his downward jabbing and upward thrusting movements. He had also just finished making his own knee protectors, which he had done all by himself. Of course I had been carefully watching him, but he did know exactly what he was doing. Toma had also cut off a hoof from the Great Hairy Beast at the last hunt, and it was this hoof that Tula worked on.

"Tula cut the hoof in half, and then set about hollowing out and shaping each half to fit each knee. When he finished the shaping he cut a hole into each protector and threaded some strong, dried gut through the hole, before winding it around his knee and its protector. His knees fitted snugly in each protector, and he tested them to make sure they stayed in place, by standing on one leg at a time and vigorously bending and shaking the other leg. Toma and I were also bursting with pride and I can remember saying to Toma, 'Look at Tula. He is so grown up now.'"

"I have seen the Great Hairy Beast," says Fasoma, "and just like Fada, I find it hard to understand how the Clan members managed to kill one each full season."

"Well that full season," says Ula, "the Clan did agree to send out an extra hunter, as well as have others standing by. We had five males, four females and Tula for the hunt itself. I was the Clan member who had to be ready with splints and healing remedies to look after anyone who had an injury.

"Of course we always did have some injuries. We certainly understood the hunt was dangerous. But really, Fasoma, in spite of the great risks involved, this particular hunt was the most important event in the full season for the Clan. The Great Hairy Beast was greatly prized for its excellent meat and bone marrow, large delicious fat layers, strong bones and tusks and the quality hides. We used every part of the animal, even its feet, as you can see."

"But now, let us get back to your hunt of the animal with soft eyes, Ula," says Fasoma gently.

"Yes, Fasoma, let me get back to my story of that special moon. As usual, Tula was in the lead, and we were down near the flat rock area, when he stopped and threw back his head, and we heard several swift intakes of breath. Tula had an amazingly sensitive nose, and he could pick up the scent of an animal long before anyone else, and even before the animal could be seen.

4

"He gave the hand signals to Toma and me to be quiet, as the animals were up ahead. We moved closer very slowly, crouching low, and made our way forward using the cover of some large trees. As you are well aware, Fasoma, we had to tread carefully so as not to make any noise, as those animals have very good hearing and startle easily with any sharp noise.

"Soon we came across a male and a female of the animal with soft eyes, having a drink in the river. Tula smiled as he gave the hand signals to be quiet and still, and so we patiently waited until the animals finished their drink and silently disappeared into the wooded area."

"Yes," says Fasoma. "*Silence is the killer. Patience is the weapon.*"

"Yes it has always been," says Ula. "*Silence is the killer. Patience is the weapon.* Anyway, we followed the two animals at a safe distance until the two met up with the others in the herd. After silently watching the herd for some time, Toma pointed out the female he had carefully selected for the kill. Tula pointed out a tree with a broad trunk further ahead, and he quietly left us and made his way around the herd and hid behind the tree.

"Toma and I waited till he was in position, and then we sprang forward and startled the animals. We closed in on the female animal Toma had selected, chasing it in a way that made it move towards the tree where Tula was hiding. The animal ran very fast, and soon after we stopped running, it also stopped to turn and look around, to see what was happening. Of course it stopped just beside the tree trunk where Tula was hiding. It was a magnificent kill, as Tula stepped from behind the tree and quickly thrust his hand spear into the animal's heart. It died instantly, without ever understanding what had happened to it."

"Yes again," says Fasoma. "*The animals are family. We kill only what we need.*"

"Yes indeed it has always been," says Ula. "*The animals are family. We kill only what we need.* We put the animal on our special sling made for three carriers, and carried it to the river to be bled. Then we proudly carried it back to the cave complex. Tula was very pleased with his killing skills, and I think that made him even more confident about his next hunt, which of course was going to be the hunt of the Great Hairy Beast.

"When we returned to the cave complex, we were greeted with beaming faces and some loud hoots of delight, in anticipation of the Clan members' favourite meat meal. It was lovely to see the Clan children all rush out of the cave as we were approaching, eager to examine which animal we had selected and killed. We had kept it a secret from them that we would be hunting the animal with soft eyes. It was a happy surprise for them.

"We carried the animal into the storage cave and placed it on the large stone and wooden bench in there. No sooner had we placed it there, than a few other Clan adults gathered around with their flints and started butchering the animal. They were quick in preparing some large chunks ready for cooking over the big fire hearth, which was already blazing. It was such a happy main meal. As I remember we also roasted fresh chestnuts that the children had been busy collecting while we were out hunting. There was a lot of laughter and happiness during that meal.

"It was the next sunrise that Toma set off to go to the far valley to see if the herd of the Great Hairy Beast had arrived yet. He was expected to camp out for one or two moons, so he carried his pouch with some freshly cooked meat of the animal with soft eyes, some chestnuts, a water pouch, a sleeping hide and his hand spear in a sheath."

Suddenly tears come into Ula's eyes, and her voice seems to falter and sound more old and tired. Ula hesitates before saying, "I remember Toma softly touched my arm and looked into my eyes. He was smiling and looking excited as he walked away, waving to all the clan members. They all called out, 'Bata bata, Toma.' We just had no idea it would be the last time we would ever see him alive. We did not know a predator had already entered our area."

The talking stops now as Ula starts crying, although neither feels embarrassed by the tears. "Perhaps next moon you can tell me more about your life in the old cave complex," says Fasoma. "I have visited it once, but that was a long time ago, and I would find it interesting to hear more about it."

Ula wipes away her tears. A faint smile crosses her face as she thinks what a sweet and thoughtful female Clan member Fasoma is. "I would be happy to tell you more, Fasoma. Just let me know whenever you have the time to listen," says Ula.

* * *

Fasoma walks away but is left thinking about all the things Ula has said. She realises that it was not so much what Ula has said that has surprised her, but it was the way she said it. Although Ula is looking old and weak, her voice is very strong and quick for someone her age. Her thoughts are also very clear too. When Ula said she remembered everything, it is now clear to Fasoma that this is certainly true. Fasoma's curiosity has been aroused now, and she genuinely wants to hear more of Ula's stories.

2

Life in the Cave Complex

Contentment is happiness,
The Clan is everything.
You never kill an animal family,
You never kill a herd.

Ula realises that ever since the talk with Fasoma, she seems to be thinking even more of past moons. Perhaps that's just what you do as you get old: think more often about the past. After all, if you are really truthful with yourself, you know there may not be much future left. So it seems more sensible to look for the good things in the past, and think of them, rather than worry about finding good things in the future.

She sighs as she thinks about her early life, and her happiness growing up in the old cave complex. "*Contentment is happiness,*" Ula whispers to herself. Life has always been very kind to her Clan members, and unlike some much earlier clans, it has been lived without any real struggle for them. The Clan has always had a plentiful food supply with all the different animal families who lived in their area. They hunt the animal with soft eyes, the animal with head bones, the animal with long tail, and sometimes the animal with fatty neck. Of course, every full season there is always the hunt of the Great Hairy Beast.

Whenever they go hunting they are always careful to regularly change which animals they hunt. It has always been this way. Central to the Clan's beliefs is the clear understanding that they have a deep responsibility towards the welfare of all the animals. They realise that this ultimately ensures the Clan's own survival. So they keep a watchful eye on the animals, and only kill what is absolutely necessary for their needs. "*You never kill an animal family. You never kill a herd,*" whispers Ula again to herself.

The animal with sharp teeth and the animal with sharp claws, which once hunted in the area, had long ago been killed by earlier clans, and so Ula's Clan members have never had any predators to trouble them. Ula nods her head, and rocks slowly. Looking back it seems to her that life in the Clan always just moved along moon by moon, much like the river itself, in an endless stream of routine but constant hard work. "*The Clan is everything. The Clan is everything,*" she repeats.

A few moons later, Fasoma approaches Ula saying, "I have fewer duties now as baba will be coming soon, so I have more time to listen to your stories. Ula, will you tell me all about the old cave complex?"

Ula notices that Fasoma's ankles are looking a little swollen, so she first advises her, "I think you need to rest even more Fasoma, and to keep your feet up when you do."

Ula makes herself comfortable, placing an extra hide behind her back, and then explains, "Well it was a very long time ago, long before I was born, that other Clan members decided to move up to the cave complex rather than live in the caves by the river."

Fasoma asks, "But the limestone cliffs down along the river are pitted with caves, giving many opportunities for shelters. Why did they choose the cave complex?"

"Certainly the cave complex was the biggest and best cave in the area, and when I lived there all of my Clan members had actually been born in that very cave complex," replies Ula. "The main cave opened up to a very large central area, with a couple of smaller caves branching off on either side. Just inside the main cave we had our big fire hearth where food was cooked and eaten, and where we held our meetings and chanting ceremonies. It was very interesting that the main cave was not completely closed at the innermost end like the caves down near the river. Our cave was different because it surprised with a round opening, which provided a clear view of the faraway valley and distant, snow-covered mountains.

"I spent a lot of time looking out at the snow-covered mountains. The other Clan members really only saw the purpose of this opening as a convenient place to throw away their rubbish and decaying matter. We were far up on top of a very steep ridge, so once something was thrown away, it was out of sight and smell forever.

"In the warmer seasons we had enough clear area outside the cave complex to erect some tent-like sleeping structures, which were made of animal hides spread across the tusks and bones of Great Hairy Beasts. It was nice sleeping outside, as we got a good cooling breeze there on the ridge top.

However, when the cooler season approached, the sleeping structures were removed, and Clan members slept inside the cave, using thick piles of hides.

"One branch of the cave had a wide opening and so still had lots of light coming in. This smaller cave served as the food storage and preparation area. It was here, at the last hunt I told you about, that Toma, Tula and I carried the dead animal with soft eyes, and placed it on the large stone and wooden bench. A large hide always lay on the floor of this cave, and this captured the butchering scraps. After the butchering was finished, a couple of Clan members would fold the hide and shake the contents outside the opening at the back of the large cave. Then the bench would be wiped down, so it was always clean and ready if it needed to be used for the preparation and sewing of the animal hides.

"In this smaller cave, the Clan also had a second and smaller fire hearth, which was mainly used for smoking animal meats and nuts, and for preparing plant remedies. We only used the second branch of the big cave, which was the smallest, for special occasions when privacy was required, such as birthing, at end of life, or when a Clan member was recovering from a serious injury and needed rest."

Fasoma interrupts Ula, saying, "But up there on top of the ridges, the Clan members lived such a long way from the river, so wouldn't it have been a nuisance always having to carry water so far?"

"Not really, Fasoma," says Ula. "We had a number of those large hide water containers that we still use this moon, so it was just a matter of any Clan member down at the river filling up one or two water pouches and returning with them to put into those containers. There would always be a number of Clan members out every moon, with each returning with one or two full water pouches, so the hide containers always stayed full.

"I remember the moon before Toma, Tula and I were leaving for our last hunt that I told you about, that the Clan children had been very busy for the last few moons, gathering up the chestnuts that had already fallen from the trees. They really enjoyed this task and it was fun watching them rushing from tree to tree collecting the nuts. As the nuts have prickles, they placed hide coverings over their little hands as they picked up the nuts. They would put them into their hide containers, which they carried over their shoulders.

"Back at the cave complex, the children came running past me, screeching with laughter, eager to see who could be first back with a full container. Myla, one of our dearest Clan elders, had just closed off the entrance to the storage cave, in preparation for smoking the nuts. He and

9

another Clan elder had trussed some hides onto the tusks of the Great Hairy Beast, and secured these in a manner to seal off the storage area.

"He was looking pleased with his preparations when some of the breathless Clan children came rushing into the cave, pushing aside the hides. I saw Myla's fair-skinned face turn into a mass of wrinkles, which all bunched up together when he laughed. He smiled kindly at the children as they handed over their containers of nuts, and he gently patted their heads as they left, calling out, 'Meta meta.' He then quickly fixed the hides again. Nothing was ever a trouble for Myla. I don't remember ever seeing him angry with anyone.

"During the next few moons, the two Clan elders were going to be busy laying the nuts out on the ground of the storage cave, ready for the smoking process, when the nuts would be left undisturbed for some moons. After that they would put the smoked nuts into large hide storage containers, ready for the next full season, just as we still do now," says Ula.

"I have heard about Myla in our chants," says Fasoma. "Tell me more about him, Ula."

"Well Myla was by far the oldest member of the Clan, and he loved to boast his age was more than five full hands of full seasons," says Ula. "But we could all see that age was certainly affecting him. His light brown hair was thinning and streaked with a whitish ash colour, as was his long and shaggy beard. After so many full seasons of hunting, his body had many scar markings, and also many broken bones that had been reset and healed.

"He had very painful stiffness in his knees, and moved with difficulty, more of a wobble than a walk. I am so thankful, Fasoma, that I have never had sore knees like Myla did. Like my hands, his hands were knotted and stiff, but surprisingly he said after time his hands became pain free. We could all see his tool making and sewing were clumsy, but that did not matter, as he really did not do these activities much anymore.

"Myla hardly ever left the cave complex, and so as not to be idle, he took over the responsibility for smoking the meats and nuts, and doing some of the cooking. I remember Myla really liked the meats most if boiled in one of our skull containers, as he found the boiled meat was much softer and easier to eat with his poor gums and few teeth. Sometimes, I would add some special herbs to the boiling water to give the meat extra flavour. Myla always gave me a special smile whenever I did that.

"Although his body was very old, the Clan members could all see his reasoning skills were still very sharp. Certainly our Clan chanting history shows just how important his reasoning skills soon proved to be."

"A couple of times you have mentioned the colder seasons, Ula. Tell me about that," says Fasoma.

"Yes, I have said how I spent a lot of time gazing out of the opening at the back of the big cave, looking at the snow-capped mountain ranges," says Ula. "I remember that this seemed to irritate Toma quite a lot, as he kept saying to me, 'Stop that constant looking, Ula.'

"But really, Fasoma, I just could not stop gazing as I was noticing how the snow and ice covering the peaks did not disappear from there, even in the warmest part of the season. The icy snow just sat on the mountain sides in long, white, finger-like formations even during the warm season. I know this sounds strange, Fasoma, but I actually was very afraid, because to me it felt as though the very coldness itself was trying to reach out and give me a warning message."

3

The Death of Toma

Always expect the unexpected.
Life always brings death.
Planning is everything.

Ula is enjoying her talks with Fasoma, and is impatient for Fasoma to join her, so she continues on with her memories as though she has Fasoma sitting in front of her. She is just starting a conversation in her mind, when Fasoma walks up to her, smiling, and sits down on a hide beside her.

"Ah Ula, at our last talk you were telling me about the cooler temperatures. Would you like to tell me more about that?"

"No, Fasoma," says Ula. "I have been thinking a lot about Toma's death, so I would like to tell you more about that first. Remember, when I was last speaking to you, I had reached the part of the story where Toma had left to go down to the big valley to see if the herd of the Great Hairy Beast had arrived for its grazing season. Well for the first couple of moons after he left, everything was normal back at the cave complex.

"But when three moons had passed and still Toma had not returned, I was starting to feel concerned. Normally he should have been away only two moons at the most, his task being just to locate the position of the herd of the Great Hairy Beast for the Clan. I said to the Clan members, 'He has never needed to stay away for three moons before, so I am thinking something has happened to him. Perhaps he may have tripped and fallen into a ravine and broken a leg, and he may be lying there unable to move.'

"After further discussion, the Clan members decided to send me out with Tula and Ola, the next moon, to search for him. We spent the whole next moon from early sunrise, searching for him, calling out to Toma whenever we passed a ravine, but there was no answer from Toma, nor was there any trace of him.

"Later while sitting around the fire at moon time the Clan's main item for discussion was Toma's disappearance. I said to the Clan members, 'We have carefully searched all the ravines now and have not found Toma. I have no idea what might have happened to him. I know if he was still alive when we called out to him, he would have called back to us.'

"'Perhaps next moon we should search in a different area and go closer to the big valley, and slowly make our way back from there,' said Tula. 'It is hard to imagine what might have happened to Fada, as he has never disappeared before.'

"So early the next sunrise Tula, Ola and I set off towards the big valley, while Soma and her partner headed out to thoroughly recheck the ravines again. We all returned at moon time but there was still no sign of Toma.

"That dark moon I couldn't sleep and was pacing around the cave. It was five moons now, and I was starting to feel panicky. I knew Tula was awake also, and so he must have heard me crying. I rarely cried then, Fasoma, and I think it was something he had only seen me do once before. That was the time when my mada had died and was buried outside the cave. Tula later told me he would never forget the look in my eyes that past moon, which he said was 'so much like the frightened and vacant stare of an animal that knows it is being hunted and has been trapped'. I just felt so lost, Fasoma. I was very worried about Toma.

"I knew Tula found it hard to see me, his mada, so upset and worried. I believe it was only just then, in the quietness of darkness, that the realisation suddenly hit him that something really dreadful must have happened to his fada. He knew then there was no other explanation for his fada's absence, and he also understood I already knew that too.

"At sunrise the Clan adults sat around the fire discussing Toma's absence, and Tula was allowed to join their discussions. It was quickly decided that three search parties would go out immediately to look for Toma. Tula spoke up, fighting back tears and sounding quite desperate. 'I want to go out again to search. I want to help my mada find my fada.'

"At that time, Fasoma, Tula was almost one full hands of full seasons, and was fast approaching adulthood. He was an excellent hunter like both Toma and me. At the time his most outstanding feature was his amazing sense of smell, something shared by his Clan members but in which he was by far the best. Because of this, he already often took the lead position when we were out hunting, as he could sniff out the animals before any of our other Clan members could.

"The Clan members decided that I should go with Tula, and head off to the far valley and stay out for two or three moons. That way we could thoroughly search that area and see if we could pick up Toma's trail. One other group would search along the river and the third group inland from the river. After some food, Tula and I took our provisions, including an extra pouch of food and water for Toma, as well as an animal hide and ties in case we needed to make a sling to carry him home.

"We spoke little as we quickly covered the ground, except to frequently call out to Toma. We had only travelled for half a light moon, when Tula stopped suddenly and started sniffing the air intently. I was wondering if he could smell a death smell, as his nose and mouth were crinkled up together as though he tasted something bitter. He raised his hand to give the 'stand still' signal. He turned his head slowly from side to side, and I noticed the expression on his face changed. He had determined which direction to go, and gave the hand signals to me to follow him with extreme caution, and to crouch low.

"A little further on he stopped again, and this time, with flaring nostrils and extra deep breaths, he sniffed the air. The smell of death was much stronger now, and even I could smell it, but I waited to see if he could detect the scent of anything else nearby. Slowly he stood up again and looked ahead. It was then in the distance that he saw a body lying in a clearing. Tula knew at once it must be the dead body of his fada. With a wild sob he rushed forward, followed closely by me. In all truth, Fasoma, I was terribly afraid of what we were going to find."

"Tell me the story about Toma's body, Ula," said Fasoma, "because I believe that it was here that you found the strange object."

"Yes," said Ula. "When we reached Toma's body, we were both badly shocked. We just shrieked and shrieked, not really understanding what we were seeing. Straight away we could tell this had been no accidental death, as we could see Toma had been brutally killed. 'Look!' said Tula, who noticed a glaring wound in his fada's stomach. 'Someone has thrust a flint spear into Fada's stomach.' Then almost at the same instant, we both then noticed there were two large dry pools of blood in the grass. Well then the shrieking started again of course.

"But the most shocking thing was what we saw next. Oh, how can I ever forget the absolute horror, as we realised that Toma's throat had been cut? This was not something we had ever seen done to a Clan member before. Almost in a whisper, covering my mouth with my hand, I said to Tula, 'Those are ugly wounds. Oh I think he must have suffered great pain.

I think your fada suffered greatly and did not die instantly.' I was quiet then, just shaking my head in total disbelief.

"Tula just stood there looking at me. He was standing in stunned silence. Later he told me that he saw my face change colour, 'looking as white as the distant snow-covered mountains'. It was then that I turned aside and was sick on the ground. I was starting to lose control, shaking and sobbing in gasping breaths. But suddenly, something beside Toma's body unexpectedly grabbed my attention. It was then, Fasoma, that I noticed a strange stone object in the long grass near Toma's body.

"The object was so unexpected, and I just had to pick it up. Looking at it, I did not understand what it was, as I had never seen anything like it before. With hands still shaking, I showed it to Tula, but he was too busy looking at his fada's wounds. He gave the object only a passing look, and just shrugged his shoulders. He also pulled a face as if to say, 'I have no idea what it is.' I showed it again, as I thought the object was important. Although I did not understand the meaning of the strange object, I realised that somehow it was connected to Toma's death."

"Finding Toma's body like that must have been really terrible for you and Tula," says Fasoma.

"Yes it was, Fasoma, but in a way it was really the start of Tula's adulthood," says Ula. "He was the one who took charge of the situation, while I just stood there. I remember noticing Tula's eyes being quickly drawn back to his fada's body. Looking at and touching his fada's body, it was Tula who determined his fada was killed the moon before. He also thought to check the surrounding area for tracks, and was surprised when he found there were four sets of tracks surrounding the body.

"'They are very large footprints, so they were probably four tall hunters,' Tula said. Even with his eyes open, Tula was able to visualise the scene. He said he could imagine his fada moving quickly in the direction of the cave complex, running into the clearing and then stopping, perhaps hearing a noise. He could imagine his fada then realising he was surrounded by the four tall hunters, as they slowly enclosed him. He could imagine one of them stabbing his fada in the stomach, and then cutting his fada's throat, after he had fallen to the ground.

"Tula then said to me, 'We should go back to the Clan at once. We do not know if the hunters might return and we have not brought any flint weapons with us.' So we quickly prepared the sling to carry Toma's body back, and gently rolled him onto the hide carrier, which we then wrapped around his body. I was feeling very nervous, imagining the four tall hunters might return at any moment. I was still holding the strange object, and so I put it into my pouch, and off we hurried.

"It was nearly mid dark moon when we returned with Toma's body. The Clan had lit fires on the ridge tops and some Clan members rushed down to help us back to the cave complex, as soon as they heard us coming. Both Tula and I were feeling totally exhausted by the time we reached the other Clan members. I think it was probably the shock of our gruesome discovery, and the grief of losing our much-loved one, that made the load of carrying Toma's body seem so unusually heavy.

"As you are aware, Fasoma, normally when a Clan member dies, the dead body would be respectfully cleaned and prepared for the burial chanting. However, so unusual were these circumstances that even at this late time of the moon, Toma's body was carried and placed in front of the central fireplace, so the Clan could examine the body and discuss what had happened. The Clan members were greatly shocked to see the cut throat, and could barely force their eyes to look at it. However, the wound in the stomach was carefully inspected.

"It was old Myla who noticed the unusual angle of the wound. He said, 'The wound in the stomach does not appear to have an upwards or downwards entry to the body as is usually made with our flint weapons. Rather it seems the flint has entered almost straight on. The wound has to have been made by a different weapon from ours.'

"It was the word 'different' that prompted me to remember the strange object I had found. So I took it out of my pouch to show to the Clan. 'This is what I found next to Toma's body,' I said, 'but Tula and I have no idea what it is.'

" '*Always expect the unexpected*,' said Myla.

" '*Always expect the unexpected*,' said the rest of the Clan members.

"Everyone's eyes opened wide, and the Clan members gasped in surprise. But again it was Myla who straight away was able to understand the significance of the object. He turned to me and said, 'Ula, it is a good thing you brought this object back to show us, as it tells us a lot about the hunters.' We were all now looking closely at the object. I noticed many eyebrows were creased or raised, and lips were pressed together and turned downwards, but we all remained silent. We were trying to work out what the object was telling Myla. None of us had any idea what it might be. It was one of those moments when the Clan was quiet but very alert, sensing Myla was about to tell us something of vital importance.

"Myla picked at two scabs on his arms. It was a diversion that gave him time to bring together his thoughts. He always said there was something very calming about picking at a scab. But the first scab came off too easily for Myla, and he looked a little irritated. He then carefully prodded around the edges of the second scab with his fingernail, gently prising it up. His eyes flashed as he appeared to experience a brief thrill, as a small sensation of pain stabbed, when the second scab was picked off. We could see Myla was pleased when a small drop of blood rose out of the indentation in the skin, slowly growing larger. He watched intently until it reached its peak, and then he smudged it with his finger. 'Yes,' he said, 'my thoughts do seem clearer now!'

"'This object is not something that has ever been made by any Clan member, as there is no chanting history of such an object,' said Myla. 'I think that we are dealing with a different people now. Judging from the strangeness of the object, I believe they must have come from a place far away.' There was a hush in the cave complex as the Clan members tried to come to terms with a situation that was so new. We had never encountered a different people before. Indeed we were not even aware that a different people might exist. This was the first time we had ever had to think of such a thing. So this really seemed to be such a new and startling thing for Myla to have said.

"Myla reminded us that in the Clan's chanting history, there had been meetings with other clans, although these had been very infrequent. In fact Myla, the eldest, was the only Clan member with an actual living memory of such a meeting. He reassured the Clan, 'Such meetings with other clans were always peaceful and co-operative, and time was spent in feasting and sharing chanting histories. As for the brutal killing, it is true that our Clan does not even have any word in our language to describe such a cruel killing as this, nor is there any memory or history of a Clan member ever killing another like this. Although there is no history of different people from far away, I think that can be the only explanation.'

"One of the Clan members, who still could not quite fathom the idea of a 'different' people asked, 'Could it be the work of the Ancient People?'

"But Myla replied quickly, 'Sightings of them are so rare, that I am not sure they are even alive anymore. Besides, we have been told in our chants that the Ancient People were always very timid and ran away, and any sightings have been of one individual, never four.'

"It was then that my own thoughts started to clear. For me it reminded me of a moment, just like stepping out of the storage cave during the smoking of the chestnuts. It's the moment when you move into the clear air of the outside area, and notice when your eyes stop tingling, and that suddenly you can see everything clearly again. I said to Myla, 'You said, Myla, this looks like the work of some different people from far away; then do you mean these people would have to be Outsiders?'

"Myla looked directly at me and said, 'Yes you are right, Ula. They would definitely have to be Outsiders. They would not be members of other clans like ours.'

"I never knew it was you, Ula, who first called these people 'Outsiders'," says Fasoma.

"Yes," says Ula, "and I will tell you it was at that very moment it struck me that life for the Clan had changed forever. I didn't say anything to the other Clan members, but somehow I just knew it."

"At the time Myla had been speaking, Tula had been busy sucking and biting his lower lip, also deep in thought. He was vividly remembering those large footprints, bigger than any he had ever seen before. This prompted him to join in. 'Yes, they are different from us, as they have such large footprints, much larger than ours. So I think they must be very tall, very tall males, I would say. I believe I know what has happened. I think my fada came across these Outsiders and was hurrying back to tell us about them, when he was ambushed and brutally killed. You can see his own weapon was still in its sheath, so he had not threatened or provoked them in any way.'

"After Tula's comments, the rest of the Clan members were still sitting in stunned silence, as no one could imagine why four tall males, who were Outsiders, would want to kill Toma, and for no reason at all! It just did not make sense to us, and yet before our eyes we could see that Toma had been killed.

"It suddenly dawned upon Myla that as the Clan members knew nothing about these Outsiders, then the Clan itself may be in danger too. He jumped up suddenly and said, 'As we do not know the whereabouts of these Outsiders now, and we do not understand why they have killed Toma, I think we need to be very careful of them. I suggest the fires be put out immediately and a watcher be sent to the ridge top.'

"After further discussion the Clan members decided to wrap the body, put out the fires, and try and to get some sleep before continuing discussions early the next rising of the sun. We were still all so stunned that we turned to Myla, as he was a Clan elder, hoping he could explain matters. But he was just as lost as we were. You see, Fasoma, the Clan just had no history of any Outsiders to help explain this matter.

"Before the rising of the sun I got up, and went to Toma's body where I gently and carefully stitched together the skin of the throat wound. I had decided during a sleepless dark moon that this had to be done. I could not allow Toma to be buried in such a state with that dreadful wound, as it would not have been respectful to his memory.

"At sunrise, the whole Clan met at the fire hearth, and a shallow grave was dug not far from the cave. Toma's body was placed in it, with some small rocks on top. In silence, I stepped forward, placed the last rock on the grave and said, '*Life always brings death.*'

"Then all the Clan members said together, '*Life always brings death.*'

"Normally a hunter's flint would be placed with the body, but on this occasion the Clan members decided to give Toma's flint weapon to Tula, his only child. They thought that perhaps now in these new circumstances each weapon could be much needed. I stepped forward again and gave the chant of Toma's life's story, telling of his deeds as a great hunter, and of his loving devotion to his family and the Clan."

"Yes, the Clan's chanting has always been such an important part of our lives," says Fasoma, "and such a lot of the time around the fire hearth is spent on memorising and retelling the Clan's chanting history."

"This is the only way the knowledge gained over many generations can be shared between the Clan members," says Ula, "and it has always been that the adult Clan members have the responsibility to try and teach the younger members everything they have learnt."

Ula drifts away from the moment, thinking more about the Clan's chants. This is something that has never changed. Always, important parts of the chanting history are presented as Clan chants, and the most important of these chants are retold as part of a Chanting Ceremony. For the Clan members this is a time of deep relaxation. While chanting, both male and female Clan members tend to speak in quiet, deep voices, that have a monotonous but soothing sound. Strangely, their voices are quite different should they become excited or alarmed, when the voices take on more of a shrill, shrieking sound. There appear to be no middle sounds to their voices.

Coming back to the present, Ula continues on with her story. "I knew that Tula had been awake all dark moon and had prepared in his thoughts a death chant to honour his fada. He stepped forward and solemnly began his chant. He had worked out an understanding of some of the events that had occurred, although he did not know the whole story yet.

"I was the last to leave Toma's grave, and just as I was preparing to walk away, I remembered Toma once telling me, '*It has been said that as we die the most important event of our life rushes before us in an instant.*'

"Standing before the grave, I whispered, 'What were you thinking, Toma, in your last instant?'

Toma's Last Instant – His Own Death Chant
For three moons I have stood silently,
Carefully watching the Outsiders.
It is a hunting party
Of four, tall, thin and dark-skinned males
With strange communication.
They are good hunters,
Quick and agile,
Cunning with their prey.
They carry flint weapons
Much like my own,
Except their weapon has a flint attached to a long stick
Which is thrown into the animal.

The Outsiders have left now
And tentatively I walk into their cave near the river.
The fire embers are cold,
And around lie the bones of small animals
Cooked and eaten.
But there in the crevice
I see something lying in the dust.
I bend over and pick it up,
What is this strange object?
It rests in my hand,
Cool to the touch like my flint,
But the edges are smooth not sharp.

It has the shape of a female torso
With big breasts and broad hips.
I have never seen anything like it before.
My brow furrows as I examine it,
It is neither weapon nor tool,
So what is its purpose?
I cannot understand it,
Nothing about it makes sense.
Why would someone spend so much time

Making an object of no practical use?
And why did they carry this object with them?
What could it be?

For a moment I feel a shiver of fear
I have never felt before.
My Clan lives in harmony with the world
Afraid of nothing.
We are fearless hunters,
And both males and females
Hunt the Great Hairy Beast.
Arms thrashing and bodies heaving,
With sharp flints
We cut soft tissue under the throat,
Until enough warm blood gushes out,
And the tired animal sinks to the ground.

Yes, I must leave quickly
In case the Outsiders come back,
Perhaps they will return for the object,
So better to go at once.
I have much to tell my Clan about the Outsiders,
My Clan will need to decide
What to do should they meet the Outsiders.
I feel certain more will come,
As I saw only male hunters,
There would have to be others close by.
Maybe I will return the object to them
When we finally meet.

I am crashing through the undergrowth
When I see a movement,
Yes, it is one of the Outsiders,
Then I realise I am surrounded.
One of them steps forward,
Cruel eyes stare at me,
And then the stick is hurled
And pierces my body.
Oh, so much pain!

The object falls from my hand.
Just like the Great Hairy Beast,
My life blood flows from me.

I know I will never see my Clan again,
There will be no warning of these Outsiders.
My Clan will wonder where I am,
And come looking for me.
They may be hunted and killed too!
I take one last look at the object,
Is that its meaning?
Is it a messenger of death for my Clan?
I should never have touched it,
Or taken it from the cave.
Perhaps that angered the Outsiders,
Who now kill me to take it back.

Ula continues, with eyes looking teary, "After the customary tears and wailing, the Clan members sat down for a quick meal and then the adults gathered for their emergency meeting. Even the children seemed nervous and agitated, aware that something very different but important was happening to the Clan. Tula was invited to join the meeting, for he would have to take on the responsibilities of an adult now and take his fada's place in the Clan.

"During the meeting, we went over and over the facts as we knew them, till an agreement was reached on what we thought had really happened. It was believed that four tall males had brutally killed Toma for no apparent reason. It was accepted that because of the angle of the wound, these males had probably used a weapon different from ours. It was known that these males had brought a strange object into the Clan's area, the purpose of which totally mystified us. All then agreed with Myla who said, 'The people who killed Toma must be Outsiders from a faraway place, who have entered our area for the first time.' Yes, we all agreed to the facts, but what did it mean for the Clan and what were we to do next?

"After much discussion it was decided that we still needed more information about the Outsiders. We needed to know if the four males who killed Toma were just a scouting party. If so, then where was their main camp, and how many others were there? We also needed information about the Outsiders' weapons and supplies, and so it was decided we would have to send out our own scouts to gather this information for the

Clan. Tula was bursting to know who was responsible for his fada's death, and he wanted to do something useful to help the Clan, so he spoke up immediately, 'I want to be a scout.'

"The Clan members always gave due recognition to Tula's exceptional sense of smell and how useful it could be. So it was agreed he should be a scout. After further discussion it was decided it would be better if he went alone, there being less chance of detection with just one person out there searching. Tula reassured the Clan about his safety, saying, 'Remember how good I was at hiding when I played hide-and-seek as a young child? No one could ever find me.' But it was still felt that this task was a big responsibility for someone who had not quite reached adulthood yet. However, in the end it was agreed that he should be up to the task. This decision was something that gave both him and me a great sense of pride.

"There was further discussion about how much danger now faced the Clan. I was always known as the thoughtful questioner, and so I was the one who said, 'Wouldn't it be wise for Clan members to move to a place further away to avoid the Outsiders?' I can clearly remember, Fasoma, that I wanted everyone to escape the danger. I wanted everyone to run away, just like the animal with soft eyes runs away from the hunters.

"But finally it was agreed that it was best for the Clan to stay in the current cave complex, as it had many sound features. It was Myla who explained to the Clan members, 'Our cave complex is at the top of some steep terrain, and is very hard to find, as well, it is difficult to approach unobserved.' Myla also suggested we keep a watcher on the nearby ridge top, to look out for any future movements from the Outsiders.

"The Clan members decided that the children would need to stay at the cave complex at all times, until Tula reported back to the Clan. Knowing we were committed to staying in the cave complex, I suggested, 'I think the adults should always work in pairs when leaving to look for food, and also all adults will need to have weapons at the ready wherever we are.' After more talk, some Clan members went down to the river to fill up some extra water hides stored at the cave. We realised it was important to have fewer trips to the river.

"Myla cautioned, 'There should be no further dark-moon-time fires in the large fire hearth that could give away our position.' With that comment I noticed a small grimace of a smile flicker across everyone's faces, as if to acknowledge our gratitude that it was not yet the cold season. Myla said, 'Some hunters will need to go out straight away to stock up on small animals for food.'

"It was then that Tula, who was looking more than a little anxious asked, 'What about the hunt of the Great Hairy Beast?'

" 'That will have to wait until the Outsiders have gone, maybe even for another moon cycle,' I replied, raising my eyebrows with just a hint of exasperation."

"I think, Ula," says Fasoma, "that last question asked by Tula was really still the child Tula speaking, and not the adult Tula."

"You are absolutely right, Fasoma," says Ula. "I do believe that Tula was nearly as distressed at the thought of missing out on the hunt of the Great Hairy Beast, as he was about the death of his fada. No one had ever missed out on the hunt before, and so he was very concerned he could not become an adult Clan member if he did not go on this hunt.

"However, I will tell you, Fasoma, that Tula grew up very quickly after that meeting. His actions after that were so brave and very important to the welfare of the Clan. I have been immensely proud of him."

"Yes I know these things, Ula," says Fasoma. "The Clan chants tell us of some of his actions."

Ula smiles fondly before continuing her story, "Although still in grief and shock over Toma's terrible death, we were still able to recover enough to manage to make some good plans. As always, we set about to approach the problems in a logical way, involving all the Clan members in the decisions."

"*Planning is everything*," says Fasoma.

"Yes, it has always been our way," says Ula. "*Planning is everything.*"

Ula is quiet now, thinking how her Clan members have been just like the many before hers, living in such a way that each adult, be they male or female, has equal importance. It has always been a good way to live, as all decisions are made only after full discussions have taken place, and agreement has been reached by all the adult Clan members. This method of making decisions has always enabled clans to live a very happy and harmonious life, with rare arguments amongst one another. The elder Clan members like Myla have always been treated respectfully, and given due recognition for their life experience and knowledge.

"And so, Fasoma, it was with the next rising of the sun that I tearfully watched Tula set off. He was proudly carrying his father's flint weapon, three water pouches and two pouches of dried meat and nuts. We expected him to be gone for half a moon cycle, but I really could not be sure I would ever see my beloved son again. All the Clan members could feel the weight of his responsibility with this task. We also realised that our future was very much going to depend on the information brought back by Tula. That is, if Tula ever came back at all."

4

The Outsiders

We should always honour the dead.
Every life is precious.

It is a nice sunny moon and Ula is resting outside on some hides, when Fasoma comes up to her. "I think this moon you will be talking about the Outsiders, Ula. Is that so?"

"Well if I really have to," says Ula. "What would you like to know?"

Fasoma is a little surprised with Ula's grumpy tone of voice, and is feeling as though she has somehow intruded into Ula's private thoughts. "It would be interesting to go over the scouts' first encounter with Toma, if it was not too painful for you, Ula," Fasoma says.

"You may not realise, Fasoma, but I have not really thought about the Outsiders for many full seasons now, and yes, it is quite painful to open up these old memories. But not as painful as Myla picking one of his scabs," says Ula, with now a hint of a smile in her eyes, trying to break the tension she has created.

"I am sorry if I was not kind to you, Fasoma, but please remember that I never managed to learn their language, and so my knowledge of their lives and what has happened are sparse."

"Ah of course, I understand completely," says Fasoma. "But, Ula, as I understand their language and have learnt much about them from my fada, then maybe you should let me be the storyteller this moon."

"That is a good idea, Fasoma," says Ula nodding and smiling. "You can be the storyteller now."

Fasoma begins, "We shall start when those four tall hunters, or scouts as the Outsiders called themselves, returned to their base camp and approached their Leader's tent to give their report. I have been told that the

Head Scout was very lively when he entered the Leader's tent to tell him what happened during the scouts' encounter with the 'Wild Man', as he called Toma.

"The Head Scout said to the Leader, 'I think the Wild Man had been watching us for a couple of moons. But whenever I looked around I never saw him, until the last moon just as we were returning home.' He described the 'Wild Man' to the Leader. 'The Wild Man had very pale skin, and at first I thought he was covered in fire ash, until I got very close to him. Then I realised it really was just pale skin. He had long, knotted, red-coloured hair, tied back, and was dressed in animal hides. He was very smelly and dirty, and quite short and stocky, but he looked physically strong and had a very well-muscled chest.'

"The Head Scout continued, 'To me he appeared a bit dimwitted, because when we ambushed him and surrounded him, he just stood there with his mouth gaping, saying and doing nothing. He did not even try to defend himself, so this behaviour appeared very cowardly to me. We had been watching him over some distance, and we noticed that although he was strong in body, he was an awkward and slow runner. He carried a flint weapon in a sheath, which he did not even try to use. I doubt if he has ever been trained in fighting, and if the rest of his people are the same, then they should be an easy enemy to overcome if we have to.' "

"Oh Fasoma, it is upsetting to hear that they spoke about Toma that way," says Ula. "To think they got everything so wrong about us all. Poor Toma, he was just curious about them, and never meant them any harm."

"Yes, it certainly is very upsetting, Ula."

"*We should always honour the dead. Every life is precious,*" says Ula.

"Yes, *we should always honour the dead. Every life is precious,*" repeats Fasoma.

Fasoma continues, "But even though this brutal killing had happened, Fada has mentioned to me on a number of occasions how fascinated the Leader was to hear about his scouts' encounter with a new and different people. Perhaps if the Leader had been there when the Head Scout saw Toma, then Toma might never have been killed."

"Perhaps," says Ula.

"Yes, we will never know that answer. Anyway, when the Head Scout finished talking to the Leader, the Leader considered the information carefully.

"He decided to send the scouts out again to try and find out more about these 'Wild People'. He wanted to know where we lived and how many of us there were. On this next trip he instructed the Head Scout, 'This time you are not to engage with them, just return with the information about them.'

"The Leader also said, 'You should first check to see if the body of the Wild Man has been discovered, and proceed with extra caution if that is the case. If the body has not been discovered then you should throw it down a steep ravine, or into the river. It is always better not to let an enemy be aware of our presence if possible, as the element of surprise is a great weapon.'"

"Yes, he was right about the element of surprise," interrupts Ula. "I do have to admit that with some matters he had clear thinking."

Fasoma can't help smiling at Ula before continuing, "The Leader had heard rumours about primitive peoples who were possibly already living in this region from ancient times, and thought Toma must be one of them. He found the combination of pale skin and red hair was interesting, as he had never come across that before. His curiosity about the new land and people had been aroused even more now, and he looked forward to the scouts' return from the next trip. It was especially good news to hear that these new people appeared to be dull-witted and cowardly, as that should make his own movements into their land so much easier to manage, and less dangerous for his own men.

"A few moons later the scouts arrived at the place where they had killed Toma. The body was gone, but the tracks showed that only two people had carried him away. The Head Scout thought that was good news, as it probably meant that the Wild People did not live too far away from this place, perhaps even within a moon's travel.

"However, they did notice there was quite a maze of tracks and pathways throughout the area going in all directions, so obviously the area had been well used for some time. Unfortunately this was going to make the task of finding the home camp more difficult. So the Head Scout decided to break up the scouting party into two groups and meet back at this place in three moons' time. One pair was to follow the river and the other pair was to head for the distant ridge tops.

"Back at the cave complex, I believe the Clan members had already filled all of their extra water hides, so that no one would now need to visit the river as was usually done each moon. The children were also back at the cave, and so this left the river area very quiet and deserted. As the Scouts moved along the river, they realised that the area was well used by people, and so the current quietness was not normal. The Wild People were obviously in hiding.

"Quite regularly the scouts diverged off the river and checked inland for a camp site, but there was no sign of one. They continued along the river for another moon before crossing over and checking the other side on the following moon. There were definitely no camps set up along the river in that area. They came across a couple of areas where they saw huge fire hearths had been set up and large animals had been butchered. But they thought perhaps the meat had then been carried off to some distant place, as there did not appear to be any permanent camp sites even near these.

"The other two scouts heading towards the ridge tops were becoming a bit irritated, believing they did not appear to be going the right way. The ground was covered with little stones that were quite slippery underfoot, particularly closer to the ridge tops. It was almost impossible to follow tracks in this terrain, and besides they found it difficult to imagine why anyone would set up camp in such an inhospitable area compared to near the river. They stumbled up and down ravines for a couple of moons, keeping a good eye open for fires and smoke at night, but seeing nothing.

"They never knew they had been spotted in the far distance, on the second moon by the Clan's watcher, who sent hand signals back to the cave complex to warn the Clan. The Clan hastily took all of the children into the far end of the big cave, and lay bushes over the fire hearth to camouflage its appearance. Some of the Clan hid behind boulders, ready to protect the Clan if necessary. But the Outsiders never really ventured close to their cave, and the Clan's watcher signalled when the danger had gone.

"The next moon the four scouts met at the prearranged site and discussed their findings. They all agreed that although there had been a lot of activity in the area, there did not appear to be a camp site of Wild People in the vicinity. They thought they would probably need to travel further upriver to find the camp. It was decided that one pair would immediately travel further up the river to continue looking, while the other pair returned to their base camp and reported to the Leader.

"Fada has told me a lot about the Leader," says Fasoma to Ula. "I do not know what Tula may have told you, so let me tell you what Fada has told me. Even though the Leader did some bad things, Ula, Fada still always had many warm feelings for him.

"The Leader, or Tibu as he was named in his village, was a person who always had a grand sense of himself and of his importance, though in truth, Fada said he actually had good reason for this healthy self-esteem. He was tall and strong, exceptionally clear-thinking, and was able to draw people closely to him. He was the first son of the most important family in their village, and his family absolutely doted on him. His grandfather had been the Village Chief, while his father was at that time the Village Chief, and it was expected that one day Tibu would become the next Village Chief.

"Tibu had grown up in a village along the sea coast in a place called Arganu, which was famous for its argan oil. Over the lifetimes of his father and grandfather, the village had developed a reputation for its fine extractions of the much-loved oil. The fruits of the argan tree were nut-sized and were covered in a thick peel, which held a fleshy pulp that in turn surrounded a hard-shelled nut. Contained within each nut were one to three argan-oil-rich kernels. An ever-growing number of the village women spent their whole days extracting the oil from the kernels, and the oil was used in many different ways for food as well as to soften the skin and hair.

"Fada explained to me that a system of trade with other villages had been slowly developing, resulting in the oil now being traded far inland. This whole idea of trade is not something our clans have ever understood or done, Ula, but it has been very interesting to hear about such a thing. It is not something our Clan is ever likely to do either, as there are no longer any other clans living close by us.

"Anyway, while still at a young age, Tibu had been the one responsible for encouraging and developing trade of the oil by sea routes to other more faraway places. This had greatly expanded the trade in the oil, and had also provided him with an opportunity to satisfy his secret desires to explore these different places. Exploring these new places was something even more important to him than developing the oil trade. Nevertheless, this boom in trade had led to more and more people moving to live in and around the village, and so its prosperity and importance increased.

"Tibu's grandfada on his mada's side was the Great Village Shaman, and so the marriage between his mada and his fada was a matter of importance and celebration in their village. It was this Shaman who had started the cult of the Mother Goddess, and this brought even more fame and fortune to the village. Since the start of the cult, the village had thrived even further with the making of stone statues of this goddess, and many new people had also been encouraged to move to the village to join in and expand this growing activity.

"Tibu had always been popular, and so it had not taken long to gather a group of admirers who were eager to please him and believed every word he said. Fada told me that Tibu had confessed to him how he was both amused and amazed by how easy it was to manipulate people to do whatever he wanted. There seemed to be no end to his power and influence over his followers, and to his natural superiority over others.

"But really, Fada admits that Tibu was different from others in his village at that time. It was Tibu who seemed to realise that the world was rapidly changing. He noticed how people were increasingly starting to move about to different areas to live, in order to have a better way of life.

"On the coastline where he had grown up, already people had been making the sea voyage across the ocean to the land of olives, for a long time. Every now and again someone returned with stories of exciting distant lands with good living conditions. As a young boy he loved to hear these stories about distant places, and couldn't wait until he was old enough to go off and explore these new lands himself.

"Having reached his maturity and having undergone the special initiation ceremony some time before, he had decided that it was time to do something brave and different. He had satisfied some of his ambitions by developing the sea trade routes for the oil, but now he wished to go much further away, really just to explore the new lands.

"He decided it was time to go, and so spoke about this matter to his five loyal friends, who said they would go with him. Tibu's fada was not pleased with this decision, but Tibu asked for his permission to spend two full seasons away, and eventually his parents agreed. His fada provided the necessary resources: a seaworthy boat, provisions of food and water, items to trade if they met other people, and two of his most trusted guards, one of whom became Tibu's Head Scout.

"Tibu returned to his village as promised in two full seasons. However, instead of being satisfied with this journey, his passion for further travel had been even more inflamed. It was apparent to his parents that he had only returned so he could get more recruits and even greater resources for his next journey.

"Tibu decided his next venture would be much grander, as he wanted to explore deeper into the new lands. So he set about securing more followers and resources. Much to his parents' alarm, he proved to be very successful in his quest of recruiting other young men as his followers. For his next grand venture, it was then that he decided to call himself Leader, and he insisted that he was always to be addressed as such by his followers, at all times.

"His parents refused to help him on this second occasion. However, he was so successful at recruiting followers and securing the necessary supplies, that it was only one and a half full seasons later that he again left Arganu by sea. He went with three full hands of its youth, many of whom were trained warriors, as well as enough provisions to last for six full seasons. Once across the sea, they travelled widely through the land of olives, which they thought was a beautiful country with good weather and plenty of natural resources. They came across small villages that had already been established by other like-minded people.

"While in the land of olives, apparently there was some trouble in the group, which resulted in one full hands of the group splitting off, some wishing to stay in the little villages to perhaps make a new life there, and others wishing to return home to Arganu. The warriors and of course the Head Scout stayed with Tibu, and he promised them all great rewards one day to repay their loyalty. After some time they reached a different countryside, where they encountered no other people, although they had heard stories about different, and perhaps more primitive people living in the area.

"Whatever you may have thought about the Leader, Ula, in his own way, he was still a thoughtful leader, in so far as he was always careful not to endanger the lives of his men. He always set up a base camp and sent out some scouts to check the next area they wished to explore, to make sure the area was safe, before the group moved into the area."

"Well it was a great pity he was not a little more thoughtful towards the Clan members, Fasoma."

"Yes, I certainly have to agree with that," says Fasoma. "So, when the Leader and his men reached the Clan's territory, Toma was the first of the different people that the Leader's scouts had encountered. They had spotted him not far from the river cave where they had slept. Realising their scouting party had probably been discovered, the Head Scout decided to hunt down and kill this Wild Man before he had the chance to warn his own people about their presence. Fada said that the scouts found the Wild Man was easy to follow as he was a slow and noisy runner, and so they actually managed to get ahead of him and wait in ambush at the clearing. They were pleased when their Leader later told them they did the right thing by killing him."

"*Every life is precious*, Fasoma," says Ula, looking very serious.

"Yes, *every life is precious*," agrees Fasoma.

"The Leader did not seem to understand that great truth," says Ula. "What sort of leader could he really be, when he did not understand that? But go back to the story, Fasoma. I shall try not to interrupt. It is just that it is always hard to hear about Toma's death."

Fasoma continues, "However, the Leader was quick to realise how important it was to know more about these different people. While he was a little disappointed the scouts had not been able to find out anything about them, he was still hopeful the pair returning from upriver would be more successful. So he was quite disappointed when the second pair also returned without ever catching a glimpse of us.

"The Leader then had to make the decision: should he set about making an all-out effort to locate the different people, our Clan of course, and check out whether or not we were friendly? Or, should he just pass through our territory into a new area and forget about us. He decided it was probably going to be too risky just to pass through our territory. He knew nothing about us, and wondered what sort of network we may have throughout the territory. He was also worried we might follow his party and ambush from behind.

"I have come to think perhaps the Leader really felt that killing the Wild Man had probably been a mistake," says Fasoma, "as after the killing, he knew it was unlikely we would wish to be friendly. However, it was too late to undo the Head Scout's actions. So unfortunately for our Clan, it was probably then that the Leader realised he would need to be prepared for a fight."

"Yes, very unfortunate for us how things worked out," says Ula. "That Head Scout was certainly a dangerous person for our Clan.

"I never thought I would say this, Fasoma, but strangely I have found it quite interesting hearing about the Leader's life. I think I have learnt more from this talk with you than I ever learnt while living with him for the whole full season."

"Ula, will you tell me what was it really like living with the Leader?"

"Well to be honest, it never felt quite real to me," says Ula. "It was like living with a shadow.

"Neither of us ever learnt the other's language, so we never talked to each other. I often caught the Leader looking at me, but I always pretended not to notice. I think there was only one time when I actually looked into his eyes. I never had any idea what he was thinking about. He was only a shadow to me, a shadow. Although I was always worried about the safety of the surviving Clan members, I was not really afraid of the Leader. You know, Fasoma, once he left, I never spoke about him again to anyone, ever, until with you just now. I could never stand to think about him, because of what he had done to our Clan."

5

Tula Observes the Outsiders

Try to expect the unexpected.

The next moon after the main meal, Fasoma is busy fussing over Ula, making sure she is warm and comfortable near the fire. Fasoma asks Ula, "Are you feeling well enough to continue with some more story now, Ula?"

"Yes, Fasoma, the next part of the story is all about Tula, and he has gone over it with me many times. It is from this part of the story that we shall hear one of his well-known chants. I am always proud to talk about Tula, especially about his courage. Let me start this part of the story."

"Yes, we were talking about the Leader and his scouts last moon, Ula," says Fasoma.

Ula now continues, "It just so happens that while the Leader's scouts were out looking for the camp of the Wild People, Tula was busy scouting the area for the Outsiders. He had decided to follow the river, as he thought the Outsiders had come from that direction. He stayed slightly inland of the river, but always kept it in sight. It was the second scouting party, as they were returning to their base camp, that he smelt coming.

"This second scouting party did not seem to be making any effort to be quiet, and so Tula climbed a large old tree to observe them. Not long after they passed nearby. He had to peer through the dense foliage to catch sight of them, and did not manage to actually see them until they had passed. He said he was amazed at what he saw!"

"*Try to expect the unexpected*," says Fasoma.

"That is often more easy to say than to do," laughs Ula. "Later when Tula returned to the cave complex he told the Clan members all about the Outsiders. We were all very curious and interested to hear about them. Tula said, 'I was greatly surprised at their appearance when I first saw them, as they looked so different from us. They were nothing like I could have ever imagined. They were very tall and thinner-looking than we are, with very dark-coloured skin and hair. They also looked extremely strong. I kept imagining how my fada must have been so interested in watching them too. I carefully followed them for the next couple of moons until the scent in the air changed. I realised there were more of them there, so I knew I had found their camp.

"'Just on dark moon time I climbed a tall tree that looked out over the camp site. A central camp fire had been lit and I could see that the Outsiders had five tent structures and one of them had a guard outside. I counted one less than two full hands of males, but felt there was still one other inside the guarded tent. Just like the two scouts, all the males were tall and dark-skinned, with thin-looking bodies, and they also appeared to be very strong.

"'There was one who was particularly tall and I think he would be nearly as tall as the Great Hairy Beast. They all had weapons attached to sheaths around their waists and the guard was holding a long stick with a flint weapon at the end. There was a stockpile of more of these near the camp fire, so obviously each man had one for his use.' It was then that Myla looked up sharply on hearing about this, and Tula caught that look. Tula stopped talking, as he needed to gulp a couple of times. He had just realised the significance of this stick weapon. It was most probably one of these weapons that killed his fada.

"Tula continued, 'I was not sure whether to watch them for another moon or two to learn more about them, or whether to return immediately to the Clan. However, I decided it was best to return and so pass on whatever important information I had. I kept thinking of the possibility that Fada was so interested in watching them when he first saw them, that he stayed around watching for too long. Besides, I realised if the Clan wanted more information then I could go back again. So just before the rising of the sun, I climbed down from the tree and this time I took the fastest route possible back to the cave complex.'"

Ula continues, "As the Clan members were holding this meeting, there was much discussion about the long stick weapons, and it was Myla who, while listening, worked out that the long stick weapon Tula saw was possibly a throwing weapon. Myla explained this by saying, 'Trying to thrust a long stick into someone does not make sense, so I think it is only by throwing it through the air at someone that the flint point would pierce the body at the straight angle.' I can remember seeing many eyebrows rising at that, as it was another new idea for Clan members to think about. But if it was true, this was vital information, because we realised that in an open space we would have no defence against such a throwing weapon.

"At the time, Fasoma, the excitement of hearing all about the Outsiders soon died away when we heard Myla's idea about the throwing stick weapon. Sometimes it can be very hard to *try to expect the unexpected.* Anyway, the Clan members all agreed that there would probably be two full hands of males, and that the one who was guarded in the tent must somehow be more important than the others. We then carefully examined our options. We had eight fit adult males, which now included Tula, and seven fit adult females. We also had five elderly Clan members, including Myla, and seven children. Should the Clan stay or run away?

"After much discussion it was decided that staying was the better option, as we could use the cave complex to hide the children and resources. Again it was Myla who spoke up saying, 'The way up to the cave complex is not easy and would make attack more difficult for the Outsiders. If they come, then we have some shelter behind the boulders near the cave, and this will provide some protection from the throwing weapons. But if we have to fight up here, there is no doubt that such a fight would be brutal and we may lose many of our Clan members.'

"I waited and let the other Clan members speak, but I was not convinced at all that staying in the cave complex was the right choice. I pointed out the greatest problem that could result from staying, by saying, 'If the Outsiders discover where we are, they could camp below us in the clear area. It would take less than a moon cycle before we would run out of fresh food and water, and then we would have to leave the cave complex to go looking for these.'

"My words brought a grim silence to the group, but the thought of leaving the security of the cave complex proved too much for them to think about. So the Clan members once again made the decision to stay. With this decision made, we immediately sent out hunting parties to gather up as much food and water as possible. We also placed a watcher on the other ridge and decided there could be no more fires at all in the big fire hearth, until we knew the Outsiders had left the area for good.

"Tula, still wanting to be useful to the Clan, suggested, 'Let me stay out in the tree area to act as a watcher for the Clan and so keep you informed about the Outsiders' movements.' The Clan members agreed to this suggestion. We all felt certain the Outsiders would come our way again. At best we could only hope that the next time we would not be found, just like the first time.

"The next rising of the sun, Tula set off to find a good place to watch for movement along the river. He was careful to stay off the main tracks in case the Outsiders sent out more scouts. He also decided only to fill up his water hide from the river at dark moon when he could not be easily seen. Later he crossed the river at a suitable place near the large flat rock, and found a high ridge top, which provided an excellent view for some distance. Not too long after, he saw the Outsiders approaching in the distance on the other side of the river. Close to them there also appeared to be a strange shape on the river itself.

"As the Outsiders came closer, Tula counted two full hands less two males, all carrying their weapons including their long stick flints. There were also two more males in a log-like structure on the water. Further up the river they stopped and set up camp for the night. The log-like structure was pulled onto the riverbank and supplies were removed from it. Tula was very impressed with their ingenuity, first the throwing stick weapon and now the floating log that had moved along the river, with the aid of two males with special wooden sticks.

"When he determined that the whole group was settled in to camp for the night and no scouts were being sent out, he decided to return immediately to the Clan and give us this important information. Again it crossed his mind that his fada probably made the mistake of staying too long to watch the Outsiders. He thought this probably resulted in his fada's discovery by the Outsiders, and then his brutal death. As Tula was aware how much more agile these Outsiders were, he knew he would need to travel during the night to keep up a safe distance and be able to stay ahead of them.

"Unfortunately for Tula, the Outsiders had camped at the large flat rock, not far from where he needed to cross the river. But he knew he would just have to take the risk and make the crossing there, as there were not many other suitable places. This spot was by far the closest to the cave complex."

"Yes," says Fasoma, "it has always been that even though the Clan lives near the river, we rarely go in the water. Past experience has taught us how dangerous the currents can be. We certainly could never afford to lose a Clan member in the river. So the river has only ever been entered to a depth where we can stand up unaffected by the current, or only ever crossed when it was shallow enough to wade across easily."

"It is so," says Ula. "Tula certainly intended to follow this custom. He had carefully noted the position of the guards, and as soon as the men had settled down for the dark moon, he crouched low in the water and quietly and slowly moved across to the other side. On reaching the other side he knew he would like to dry out his hides, as he was feeling quite cold, but he realised there was no time for that now. Once he was at a safe distance from their camp he headed back to the cave complex as fast as possible. He arrived back at the cave breathless and exhausted, and feeling miserable in his wet hides. Once more, the adults called a Clan meeting to decide what should be done after hearing this latest news.

"Fasoma, I can clearly remember that after Tula's return, I was feeling even more anxious about the Outsiders, and still really wanting the Clan to leave the area."

"I wonder if that would have saved their lives, if they had done that?" Fasoma asks.

"I am afraid that is another question that will never have an answer," says Ula. "I strongly urged all the Clan adults, 'We should take a few belongings and leave immediately. Once we reach the river we can head inland, and go towards the big valley where the Great Hairy Beast arrives. It does not look like the Outsiders will backtrack, as they seem to be heading upriver and towards our area.' However, once again the Clan members showed their reluctance to leave the cave complex and decided to stick with the original plan. Myla could be very persuasive.

"After further discussion amongst the Clan members, I accepted their decision. I had still been quietly thinking about the Clan's safety, and so I suggested, 'Perhaps Tula should act as an extra watcher and stay outside of the cave complex down in the tree area. As we are uncertain of the Outsiders' intentions, then having someone watching them closely will be very useful.' The Clan adults liked this idea and agreed to it. The next light moon, Tula headed down to the tree area and chose a suitable place to hide, so he had a good view of the river and the pathways.

"He had only just settled in when he spotted the strange floating log coming round the bend in the river. This time there were three men in it, and the one in the middle, the incredibly tall one, was carefully turning his head from side to side watching the shore, while holding his throwing stick erect.

"The floating log moved on further up the river and disappeared out of sight. Later in the moon, Tula heard the other men approaching. He had hidden not far inland from one of the old hunt hearths. He had thought he would be safe there, because he knew that this area had already been well searched earlier by the Outsiders. Unfortunately for Tula, it was purely a matter of coincidence that the Leader decided he would move his base camp up to one of these river sites the scouts had mentioned seeing earlier, and from there send out scouting parties.

"So it was with horror that Tula watched the Outsiders approach the hearth and start to set up camp. He understood how easily he could be trapped, as the Outsiders only had to venture out for firewood to discover him. He has since told me that at the time he felt very afraid. He lay down as flat as possible on his stomach, and placed some brush bushes over himself and waited for the cover of darkness.

"It was not long before a couple of the Outsiders moved close by gathering wood, just as he thought they might. He said he could feel his chest pounding as he lay very still, almost too afraid to take a proper breath. But the two Outsiders didn't seem to see him, and they returned to the camp. A short time later before he heard their approach, he picked up their scent. Then before he understood what was going on, some men had thrown a rope structure over him, in which he became hopelessly entangled. Then three men pounced on top of him and managed to take away his weapon. Within no time his arms were tied behind his back with rope, and a strange contraption was put around his neck, before he was roughly led back to their camp.

"Tula had never before seen a rope structure like the one thrown over him, and again he was surprised by the ingenuity of these strange people. Even though in fear of his life, he said how he still managed to wonder if such a rope structure could be useful to help capture some of the animals hunted by the Clan members, as they did not have anything like it. This would certainly be something to consider in the future should he manage to escape. But then reality hit him, the undeniable fact that they had managed to capture him so easily. This realisation gave him grave fears not only for his own safety, but also for the very Clan itself.

"He was pulled by a rope attached to the contraption around his neck. If he struggled against the Outsider pulling, or fell down, then the contraption seemed to tighten and he felt as though he was choking. When he and the Outsider reached the Leader, the Leader stepped forward and in harsh tones attempted to communicate with him. But Tula could not understand a word the Leader was saying, and could barely talk himself, as the contraption round his throat was still making it hard to breathe properly. Then the Leader seemed to issue a command and one of the Outsiders rushed over and loosened the contraption.

"For some time the Leader attempted communication with Tula, with a mixture of speech and sign language. Tula realised he was being asked where the Clan lived, but he pretended to have no idea what the Leader was asking. Finally the Leader cleared a patch of dirt at his feet and used a stick to make a rough outline of the river, showing the distant ridge tops and the current fire hearth. Tula was dumbstruck. None of his Clan members had ever made such markings in the dirt, and he realised that looking at the markings was just like looking at a story being told in the dirt. So right here before his eyes was another good idea the Clan could use. Obviously, he thought, there was a lot that could be learnt from these Outsiders, and there was much to tell the Clan members if he could manage to survive and get back to them.

"The Leader, looking impatient, raised his voice in a threatening manner and pointed to the markings in the dirt. Tula just gazed at him with large blank eyes, not making a sound. The Leader became enraged, and stepped forward and hit Tula across the head. Tula fell over and felt his breath being cut off, as the contraption pulled on his throat. This process was repeated a number of times until the Leader gave a new order, and Tula was taken away and tied up to a tree. He was left standing there all dark moon and was not offered any food or water."

"He showed a lot of courage, Ula, going through such a frightening experience," says Fasoma. "Certainly, according to our chanting history, no other Clan member has ever been captured and tied up before, and treated so badly."

"Yes," says Ula, "I am not really sure if any of our other Clan members would have had so much courage. It was really amazing that he was able to still think of the Clan's welfare at a time when his own life was under threat. Especially knowing these people had already killed his fada.

"Anyway, the next moon Tula said how he was largely ignored, and that he noticed small scouting parties heading out in different directions. Towards dark moon time, he was offered his first drink of water, but still no food. His legs were aching by then, as were his shoulders, and his hands were hurting badly, still tied behind his back. He had spent the whole dark moon wiggling the rope to try and free his hands, but the rope, once wet with his blood, only seemed to tighten further and cut more deeply into his flesh.

"Later, in the light moon, he saw the floating log return with its three occupants, and most of the other scouts came back soon after. The Leader talked to them. Shortly afterwards a guard loosened the ropes that tied Tula to the tree, and he felt so weak that he fell to the ground. Two guards then dragged him to the Leader. They again went through the charade where the Leader pointed to the markings in the dirt, obviously asking where Tula's

Clan lived and how many people were living there. Tula continued to just stare at the Leader with large blank eyes, only this time he was thankful he was not beaten or choked.

"Finally he was dragged back to the tree and tied up again, and given his second drink of water. Then at dark moon, his hands were untied and he was given his first meal. The Leader and the others seemed to have lost interest in him by then, and Tula was quick to come to the understanding that he had been given an important opportunity to watch and learn about these Outsiders. So he set about to carefully observe all their routines, and how they went about their activities.

"Again," says Ula, "every time I think of this story I am amazed at how adult Tula's behaviour was. I am not sure even I could have acted with so much courage under those circumstances."

"You are underestimating your own courage, Ula," says Fasoma. "I know as the story progresses your courage becomes its own legend."

Ula smiles at Fasoma's kind words. She is really quite pleased to hear this said about herself. Ula continues on with her story. "Apart from the throwing stick weapon, Tula noticed their tools were very similar to those of the Clan, and all of their clothes and shelters were made out of animal skins too, albeit different animals. The Outsiders were tall and strong and looked different from our Clan members. They communicated with a different language, but interestingly Tula already understood a few words of their language. Many times he heard the word 'prisoner' and he knew that referred to him.

"Tibu, the Leader, must have realised that his prisoner had not yet reached manhood. Although he probably believed Tula was about one full hands and six full seasons. The Leader was perhaps not sure whether the prisoner's refusal to answer his questions was a sign of his complete stupidity or a show of an admirable courage for someone so young. His men had thought the original man they killed was quite stupid, so the Leader accepted that perhaps this was the way we really were.

"Although noticing the prisoner was dirty and unwashed, the Leader would have never seen a person with such pale skin before. He may have even thought it was a coincidence that in his own initiation ceremonies back home, the Shaman covered the bodies of the young males in fire ash, which gave them a similar pale appearance to this prisoner. It might have crossed his mind that the Mother Goddess statue also had a pale appearance, as it is carved out of white stone. Perhaps he even believed there was a special importance to a pale skin colour, one that he had not realised before, something the Shaman had known about but not shared with others.

"The Leader apparently thought it would be sensible not to kill his prisoner at this stage, but to keep him as a prisoner, as he may prove useful at some later time. So Tula, still with the contraption around his neck was tied with a rope to the tree, so that he was still able to lie down, and was then offered food and water two times each moon. He was not considered a threat to their party, so no one paid much attention to him anymore.

"The Leader's men had camped by the river for over a half moon cycle, and still there had been no sign of the prisoner's people. The Leader's log boat had travelled quite a distance up the river with the scouts, who had now searched extensively along both sides of the river. The ravines were so steep and impassable, that no one believed anybody would live up there. Still, it did not make sense to the Leader that one as young as the prisoner would be roaming the countryside on his own.

"Some of the Leader's men had also explored a few of the caves along the cliff face, but they noticed these did not appear to be in use. The Leader decided to wait another seven moons until the full moon before moving on. He had not decided yet what to do with the prisoner once they moved on.

"Fasoma, could you explain a little about the worship of the Mother Goddess?" asks Ula. "Tula did explain some things, but I do not really remember them much."

"Yes, Ula, I am happy to tell you about that, as Fada has spoken about it often."

Fasoma says, "Back at the Leader's home village, each full moon the Shaman would hold a special ceremony to honour the Mother Goddess. On such an occasion, each villager would bring a gift of thanks to the Mother Goddess, and these gifts would be placed inside a special tent erected for the purpose. During the dark moon, the Shaman would hold a ceremony to intervene on behalf of the villagers for their continued good health and welfare. This was followed by a feast prepared by the village females, and after this there would be much singing and dancing around the fire, sometimes even all dark moon.

"Whenever someone in the village had a special problem, the person could go privately to the Shaman, and ask him to intervene with the Mother Goddess on their behalf. The Shaman could demand a gift for such a special intervention, the value of which depended on the type or seriousness of the problem, and also what sort of valuable goods the person could offer.

"Every family in the village was expected to keep a stone statue of the Mother Goddess in their home, so that the Mother Goddess would know they were true followers. If something bad happened in the village, the Shaman would say that the people had not been showing enough devotion to the Mother Goddess. Thus they would need to provide even further gifts to please her.

"On the whole, the people in the Leader's village viewed the Mother Goddess as a good thing to have, as she was helpful and comforting to the village people. This ready acceptance of her special qualities and abilities to help them personally, allowed the cult to develop quickly and become part of everyday life in the village.

"Meta, Fasoma, for that," says Ula, "But I still find the idea of a Mother Goddess such a strange thing. Now getting back to when the Leader was holding Tula a prisoner, there was a full moon approaching, and unfortunately there was no Shaman available for the Leader's men in this area. So the Leader decided he would hold an intervention ceremony to the Mother Goddess himself. This would be the first time he took on the role of Shaman and he would ask the Mother Goddess to help him find the Wild Peoples' camp. I am sure the anticipation of such an important step as being a Shaman made the Leader feel very powerful. I know your fada once said that the Leader had told him how he could feel his heart was pounding, while his mind seemed to be on fire.

"You must let me tell you Tula's chant now," says Ula to Fasoma, her face lighting up markedly now. "It is one of my favourite chants. It tells of all the things we have just talked about, and even more still."

Tula's Chant While Being Held a Prisoner by the Outsiders

The Scouts have come and gone
A number of times,
Searching for my Clan along the river.
I can see the frustration on their faces
When they return
With nothing to report.
Perhaps they will leave soon
And life will go back to normal again.
I can see the Leader
Is becoming impatient,
And I wonder what will be my fate?
I just cannot tell.

In the sky there is a full moon and
The Leader comes out of his tent
Holding high an object.
I strain to see the object,
Yes, now I see what it is.
It is the female torso
With big breasts and broad hips.
It is the same as the object found by my mada
Next to the body of my dead fada.
Perhaps I will now learn
The mystery of its purpose,
This object of death.

The Leader cries out and
The men step forward one by one
And lay an item at the Leader's feet.
They are presenting a gift
To this lifeless stone.
How strange is that?
A stone cannot speak
A stone can give nothing,
And yet I see how much the object means to them.
They are all chanting wildly, and
The Leader's face is in raptures,
Perhaps for them the object means life.

Their movements are interesting,
As my Clan never moves like that.
I watch their bodies swaying in unison
Like grass reeds in the breeze,
Side to side.
Their chanting voices
Building to a high crescendo,
Then they jump up and down.
Flashing eyes glazed yet on fire,
They twirl and twirl around
And finally fall to the ground,
Exhausted, then asleep.

The next moon there is
Great commotion in the camp,
Two scouts return animated
And head straight for the Leader.
I have a sense of foreboding,
That all is lost,
They have found the Clan's cave.
The Clan will be trapped and killed.
Oh how I hate the stone object,
It is the messenger of death.
Oh, so much pain!
Just like a spear through the heart.

"It was good to say Tula's chant again, but perhaps, Fasoma, you can now continue on with a little more of the story and let me have a rest," says Ula.

So Fasoma continues, "I have heard from my fada that the Leader was very pleased about his intervention ceremony with the Mother Goddess the moon before. The next moon, the Leader laughed aloud about his good fortune when the scouts returned with the news they had found the camp site of the Wild People. The Leader totally accepted that his intervention ceremony had been the reason they had found it, and so had been a real success. It was just amazing too, as this was the last time he was sending out the scouts before moving on. Yes, the Mother Goddess had definitely listened to him and answered, the Leader thought. Now indeed he believed he was a true Shaman, with a Shaman's real power.

"The two scouts reported to the Leader. One of them said, 'We had just left the river, and were sitting behind a tree when we heard a little rustle in the grass. We watched a pale-skinned male and female carefully approach the river, and bend over at the water's edge to fill some hide containers with water. The containers were large and heavy to carry when full, and so the pair struggled back along the path. As they were quite noisy, it was easy to follow them at a safe distance. We were surprised when we realised they were heading up towards the ridges. This time we travelled for a much longer distance than on previous searches, and we carefully noted any landmarks along the way.'

"The scout continued, 'At one point, the two of them actually left the track and veered behind some large boulders that led to a heavily wooded area. When we passed through this area we came to a clearing, and then followed a track that led steeply uphill from there. Some distance on, just before we turned a bend in the path, we realised that the two ahead had stopped, so we climbed behind a boulder to the side and peered ahead. There on the ridge further ahead we saw a sentry, and even though we could not yet see the camp, we knew we had found their camp area. So we returned immediately to tell you.'

"The Leader realised his men probably would never have found the camp except for this lucky encounter with the two collecting water. But it was the Mother Goddess who had made this encounter happen, he thought. His men understood this also, and so to his men, finding the camp of the Wild People was proof that the Leader's intervention with the Mother Goddess had been a magnificent success.

"This all now affirmed his new status as Shaman as well as their Leader. To the Leader, the success of the intervention meant the Mother Goddess must have wanted him to find the camp of the Wild People, although he was still not quite sure for what purpose exactly.

"However, the Leader was quick to recognise his new status, and that evening he made a hole in the Mother Goddess statue and threaded a thin rope through it. He decided that, just like the Shaman back in his village, he would proudly wear this powerful symbol around his neck at all times. That night around the camp fire, there was much singing and dancing again, as the men all paid homage to the Leader and the Mother Goddess.

"The next day the Leader set off with a party of five, deciding this time he would like to go himself. They went as far as the bend in the path and the Leader decided not to proceed further but instead to make their way across to another ridge in the distance, which he thought might overlook the camp. He did not know it, but his party had been spotted by a Clan watcher on the ridge, the moon before and again just then. The watcher realised what the Leader was about to do and scampered down a ravine and hid until the Leader passed at a safe distance. The Clan watcher then rushed back to the cave complex to warn the Clan.

"When the Leader reached the ridge, he had an excellent view of the Clan's cave complex. Although there were no people to be seen, he was sure they were hiding in the large cave he could see, while some could also be hiding behind boulders. The Clan members had attempted to camouflage the fire hearth inside the cave with some brushes, but it was easy to see the ground was covered in numerous tracks and cast-off flint stones. Inside the cave, he could even see some hide tent structures, which the Clan had hastily moved inside just the moon before.

"The Leader realised it could be a costly exercise just to rush in and attack, so he left two men as sentries on top of the ravine. They were left with light provisions, and the Leader and the others headed back to his camp site. The sentries' task was to watch the cave area and try and determine how many people lived there. The Leader was heartened as he felt the group could not be too big.

"It was also immediately obvious to him that the Wild People would be vulnerable to a lack of food and water, living up there on top of the ridge. The very fact they took such a risk to collect water at the river so recently showed they were probably already running very low on water supplies. It was looking as though the Mother Goddess had intervened in this way because he was meant to find their cave.

"Yes, it seemed a good strategy to deprive the Wild People of their access to the river and hunting. Maybe later, in a weakened state, the Wild People might surrender or else be easily overcome. On the way back to his camp, the Leader selected a clear area where he would set up a new camp for his men, and move them much closer to the upcoming action. Two scouts would stay at the river camp with the prisoner, and it would also be their job to carry fresh food and water supplies up to his new camp, and to the sentries on the other ridge."

6

The Outsiders Are Predators

We must live with what we do.

Feeling rested, Ula takes over telling the story. She says to Fasoma, "Once our watcher had returned from the ridge top after spotting the Outsiders moving up the ridge, the Clan members realised what a terrible situation we were in. Now the Clan would have no way of gathering information, other than by leaving the safety of the cave complex. We had already brought in the hides of the Great Hairy Beast and set up some tents inside the cave. This gave us some privacy from the prying eyes of the watchers on the ridge. We gathered behind these tents to have a meeting to try and work out what we should do next.

"At the time of this meeting I was feeling very upset. I still believed my instincts for the Clan to run away when the Outsiders first appeared were the right ones. Twice previously I had urged the Clan to leave the cave complex, but the other Clan members just did not seem to see the danger that was so obvious to me."

"Perhaps you just sensed the danger more, Ula, because after all, you were the one who had personally suffered the greatest losses with Toma's death and Tula's disappearance."

"Yes, Fasoma, I think you are right," says Ula. "I can remember how my body shook when I first saw Toma's dead body. It was such a dreadful shock. I had this urge to run away, but then I realised, if I were to run from a predator, it would probably just chase me anyway.

"During our meeting, the Clan members decided to place two watchers of our own beside the pathway leading up to the cave complex. One elder member volunteered for this role and we decided the other watcher would be one of the young females – Suta, who was the Clan's fastest runner. Myla thought it was probably the gathering of the last water supply that gave away our position to the Outsiders. At the time, Fasoma, I believed he was probably right. And now we know that is what happened. I think we gave the two water carriers a container that was too large and too heavy, and it was hard for them to bring it back. They felt terrible about it, thinking they had been careless, but it was too late for anyone to change something that had already happened."

"*We must live with what we do*," says Fasoma.

"Yes indeed," says Ula. "*We must live with what we do*. We discussed our supplies, and realised that even if we rationed our water, we would still only have enough for half a full moon cycle. Although we were now practically out of fresh meat, we still had plenty of nuts and some smoked meats and fats, and could stretch this out for easily a full moon cycle or more. The shortage of water was the real problem.

"To us it looked as though the Outsiders were probably going to attack, but most likely they would wait until they thought the Clan had run out of food and water. Again, I was the one who brought up the possibility of leaving the cave immediately. I felt I just had to suggest it one more time. Only, when I did this time, I was feeling desperate. I said, 'We should take our weapons and some food and water, and leave right now before the Outsiders have an opportunity to get organised below. This will be our last opportunity to leave and escape from the Outsiders. But we need to leave right now.

" 'We could break up the Clan into family groups, and could scatter out in the tree area and hide there, and some could make their way to the big valley. It will be just a case of luck as to who is hunted and killed and who survives. For sure some will die but also some will survive. If we stay here we may all die. But if we go, it must be at once.'

"The Clan adults were quiet after I said this. They considered this plan, but I could see most of them felt they really wanted to stay together. They avoided making eye contact with me. They were half nodding their heads but actually saying nothing. Myla understood their mood, and spoke up for them. 'Our strength has always come from working together. I do not believe the Outsiders intend to just go away, so a fight does look inevitable. I think it is better to all fight together. We are strong and will be good fighters.' So it was very unfortunate, but the Clan members made the final decision to stay in the cave complex.

"We decided that when the time came, the children were to be taken to the little cave where I was to be put in charge of their defence. If a struggle ensued, then I was still not to leave them to fight with the others. I had to stay with the children, as I was to be the last line of defence for them. We discussed where other Clan members would position themselves should an attack occur.

"So you see, Fasoma, I had no choice but to accept whatever the Clan decided. There was no time for concerns about whether or not the others had made the right decisions. It is just our way of doing things, that the Clan members accept joint responsibility for our decisions. But I can tell you that the next one full hands of moons seemed to last a lifetime. It was terrible.

"The Clan members could not avoid seeing the two Outsider watchers on the other ridge top. They lit fires at dark moon, and during the light moon taunted us by holding up fresh game. Even from this distance we could smell the odours of the Outsiders' freshly cooked meat. Further down the pathway, where the rest of the Outsiders were camped, we could see their camp fire lit at dark moon, and could hear their wild shouting and chanting. While in the cave complex, it seemed that the Clan members hid away in darkness, talking only in whispers.

"The situation in the cave complex was becoming very grave as the Clan members realised we were running out of water. Everyone was tired and irritable, and even the children were complaining about the lack of fresh meat and not having enough to drink. It was obvious to everyone that something needed to be done. I could no longer stand doing nothing, and so I called another meeting. In anguish I said, 'We cannot just wait in the cave to die of thirst; we have to do something soon. If we are going to die, then let us die fighting.'

"Discussions were tossed to and fro, and finally it was Myla who suggested, 'Let us send out two elders, with no weapons, just with two empty water hides to ask for water. Let us clearly show the Outsiders that we do not want to fight them, but are peaceful.'

"Ata volunteered, 'Let me and my partner go, as we are too old to fight anyway.' And so it was decided that at sunrise Ata and her partner would go down to the Outsiders' camp.

"When the time came and the two Clan elders were leaving the cave complex, it was with heavy hearts that we waved to them, saying, 'Bata bata.'

"The two Outsider sentries on the ridge top obviously noticed the two Clan elders leaving. They immediately lit two fires. Apparently their agreed signal being, one lit fire on top of the ridge meant a fighting party, two lit fires meant a peace party on the way. I am sure the Leader smiled to himself when he saw the two fires, as he knew he had been right when he thought that in half a moon cycle the Wild People would be out of water. To him it must have looked as though the Mother Goddess had really wanted the Wild People to die after all.

"The Leader allowed the two elders, one male and one female, to walk into his camp, and he observed they were not carrying any weapons. Instead they held two empty water containers out in front of their bodies, in a pleading manner. The Leader must have thought there was something quite pathetic about the Wild People's behaviour, and so he said to the Head Scout, 'Let us send back a strong message to the others.' He ordered the Head Scout to kill the elderly male immediately. Poor Ata was handed the two empty water hides and pushed roughly back in the direction of the cave complex.

"She started sobbing and screeching, and was almost hysterical when she returned to the Clan. She told us what had happened. I could see the Clan members were starting to look panicky just like Ata. They all started screeching too. I spoke up in a loud voice, saying, 'There must be quietness. We need to hold a meeting. Quietness everyone.' When the adult Clan members finally settled down enough to discuss the matter, I noticed Myla was strangely quiet. It was such a sad moment, Fasoma, as the Clan members were at a complete loss to understand this brutality of the Outsiders.

"However, we were left in no doubt of our future. We had clearly understood the dreadful message from the Outsiders. There would be no peace and no mercy for us. Once we recovered from the initial shock, then a profound sense of outrage overtook each Clan member. It was with an icy resolve that we then discussed our next action. Up to that moment, I had always been the one who had thought the Clan should run away from the Outsiders, but suddenly I saw things very differently.

"Yes, Fasoma, I will say that it was only then that I finally grasped the situation for what it really was. So what I did next was to completely change my mind. I had been remembering the Clan's chanting history that spoke about times in the faraway moons, when some clans had been troubled by predators, like the animal with sharp teeth. These chants told how whenever these predators came howling into the Clan's land, then the Clan members would immediately send out a hunting party to kill them.

"Well I realised these Outsiders were the same. They were nothing more than predators of the Clan. They too must be killed. We had to do this, not only for the Clan's safety, but also now for its very survival.

" '*The Outsiders are predators,*' I said in a firm voice.

" 'Yes,' said Myla, also in a firm voice. '*The Outsiders are predators.*'

"All the adult Clan members repeated the words in forceful voices. '*The Outsiders are predators.*' The Clan members knew exactly what had to be done to predators. So the decision was made very quickly.

"We decided to send out a fighting party to attack and kill the Outsiders the very next moon. It was Myla who said, 'We should start this attack well before sunrise, under the cover of darkness. At least this will deny the Outsider watchers the opportunity of lighting their warning fires.' The Clan decided again that I would stay in the cave to guard the children. The other elders were to hide behind the boulders, ready for fighting should the Outsiders approach the camp. Myla asked to be allowed to accompany the fighting party, and although it was considered unusual for someone his age, permission was given for this request.

"When this decision was made, a real calmness seemed to descend upon the cave complex. Strange that this should be so, as it was the very first time the Clan members had ever made a decision to kill a predator, let alone another person. We busied ourselves checking our weapons, talking and even laughing together, before having an early meal. We lit the fire and all sat down after the meal to chant our Clan history.

"Each of the Clan members, including the children, was allowed to recall his or her history and memories. We knew this was going to be the last occasion we would all be together. The next moon we would no longer all be alive, so we clearly understood that each moment now together was very precious.

"It was then that I took the strange stone object and made a hole in it, and threaded some animal gut though the hole. I tied it and hung it around my neck. Somehow, having the object on my body made me feel closer to Toma, whose lifeless body was found beside it. With some tears in my eyes, I also thought of my son, Tula, who was with me at that time and was now missing. He was most probably killed too, by these Outsiders.

"I know none of the Clan members had understood the purpose of the object, but who could possibly understand these Outsiders anyway? Tula had called it 'an object of death', so how appropriate then to wear it the next moon. I would soon find out if death was its purpose."

While talking about the Mother Goddess statue with Fasoma, Ula has become aware that a number of the younger Clan members seem to be hanging around the fire hearth. They are listening in, of course. Ula can't help but smile. She thinks how funny it is to watch those listening in on a conversation when they are pretending not to. They don't realise, but their body movements seem to slow or stop altogether, and even their eyes stop blinking. Their heads seem to lean forward, while their breathing quietens too. She notices some actually hold their breath when she is saying something they think is important. Obviously the Clan members are interested in her stories too, but they just haven't said so.

She thinks maybe next moon she shall invite them to join the talks. She doesn't think Fasoma will mind; after all, her story really belongs to all the Clan members. She will speak to Fasoma after this talk finishes. Next moon, she will tell them all about the Clan's fight with the Outsiders, because it was and will always be such an important event in the Clan's history.

Ula continues, "While the Clan members were making their preparations, down in the Leader's camp the Leader had also been busy preparing for battle the next moon. The Leader knew the Wild People must be almost out of water, and so should be desperate by now. He decided that if the Wild People did not attack after sunrise then he would move up to the cave later. Either way it would all be finished long before the dark moon.

"He sent a runner to the sentries on the ridge to tell them to return to his new camp after sunrise if there was no activity at the cave. He also sent a runner down to the river camp to send up the two guards from there. That light moon around his camp fire, he held a special ceremony to the Mother Goddess for a good victory the next moon.

"Tula had been left securely tied to the tree, again with the terrible contraption around his neck. The guards had left him with only a container of water. He had watched the runner from the ridge camp arrive and talk to his two guards in a very animated fashion, and he understood then that the fighting would be the next moon. He had already observed them hunting and carrying food and water the past moons, obviously to the Leader's other camp. It was not difficult to work out that they must have camped below the Clan's cave, to prevent the Clan members from leaving to obtain food and water. He only hoped his Clan was still fit and would be ready.

"When the Leader and his men went to sleep that dark moon, we have been told that the Leader was apparently feeling very confident about victory the next moon. So far he had seen no evidence that the Wild People were interested in engaging in any sort of fighting. He probably thought we were just timid people who were cowards after all, and so really did not deserve to live. He may have believed the Mother Goddess had known this, and the next moon should grant him an easy victory."

7

The Clan Fights the Outsiders

Silence is the killer,
Surprise is our hunting friend.
Ula and Soma have so much courage.

Later the next moon, Fasoma tells Ula that now all the Clan members want to come to the next talk. They are all very interested to hear Ula's story about the fight with the Outsiders. After the main moon meal, Fasoma busily arranges hides around the entrance of the cave. She stacks a thick pile of hides, trussed on some tusks of the Great Hairy Beast, near the fire hearth. She smiles to herself. Yes, Ula will be able to sit up in comfort, resting her back, near the warmth of the fire while facing the Clan members, as she tells them her story.

The Clan children sit cross-legged on the front hides, while the adult Clan members gather behind. There is almost an air of excitement when Ula sits down in front of them all. Just before she starts to speak, one of the Clan children asks, "Ula, why doesn't the Clan have a Clan chant about the fight with the Outsiders?"

Ula is stunned by this question. This is the first time this matter has come to her attention, and for a moment she is lost for a reply. Fasoma starts to say something, but Ula raises her hand and says, "I think it is better if I try to answer the question. Yes it is true. The Clan does not have a chant about the fight with the Outsiders. This must seem very strange to you, and I am sorry but I do not really have an answer. I can only suggest that we look at the history of the fight, and then maybe after that, we can work out the answer to this question. But for now, let us go back to the dark moon just before the fight began.

"Up in the cave complex, the Clan was in luck as there was a thick cloud covering, and so there was no real moonlight when the Clan adults quietly left the cave, one by one. They felt confident that the Outsiders' watchers on the other ridge would not now see them in the darkness. It had been a good idea of Myla's – to leave in darkness. So it was still well before the rising of the sun when they quietly made their way along the rocky pathway that they knew so well.

"They had seen the Outsiders' camp fire, so they knew exactly where the Outsiders would be camped, down in the clear area. Hopefully now they would all be sleeping. Certainly everything was very quiet. The Clan members believed the Outsiders would have a guard somewhere along the track and so they proceeded with great caution. The Clan member in front picked up the scent of the guard, and the signal was sent back along the line.

"Realising the guard was asleep, and that it would be better not to risk trying to kill him and perhaps making a noise that would alert the camp, the lead Clan member gave the hand signals to those behind. So one by one they silently moved around the sleeping Outsider guard and passed by. Further along the path, Myla signalled that once he had passed the guard he would stay nearby in hiding. Myla understood that once the fighting started, then the guard would wake up and come running along the pathway back to his camp. Myla wanted to be waiting for him.

"As you are aware," says Ula to the listening Clan members, "the Clan members often use this same strategy when hunting, and always with great success. Two or three hunters will creep up towards the animal with soft eyes or another animal, and startle it. The poor frightened animal will speed away, usually only for a short distance, and then stop, panting and watching behind. It will never see the extra hunter already hidden behind the nearby tree or boulder, or sometimes even hidden in the tree above. Over the many hunting seasons, and with much hunting experience, all the Clan members have a good idea how far each different animal will run before it stops to look back.

"Anyway, with Myla well hidden, the rest of the Clan members continued down toward the Outsiders' camp area. When they reached their camp site, all was quiet and the camp fire was only a few burning embers. Some of the Outsiders were asleep on the ground, while others were asleep in the tents. The Clan members signalled in turn which tent or male they were heading for.

"We are lucky that the Clan has more than three full hands of different hand signals we can use when hunting," says Ula, getting a little sidetracked again. "Quietness is such a crucial part of our hunting strategy. *Silence is the killer.*"

"*Silence is the killer,*" repeat all the Clan members.

"*Surprise is our hunting friend,*" says Ula.

"*Surprise is our hunting friend,*" say all the Clan members.

"Well, the first moment the Leader must have realised that his camp was under attack was when he heard the guard outside his tent scream out in pain. He jumped up and grabbed his weapons, shouting out to his men to do the same. Outside the tent he was confronted with a female Clan member fighting his guard, and the guard appeared to be losing the battle. As soon as she saw the Leader, the Clan member left the guard and lunged at him. The Leader only just managed to sidestep her at the last moment.

"The camp was in turmoil and it was hard for anyone to see what was happening in the darkness. The Clan members had a short period of advantage as their eyes were accustomed to the darkness, while the Outsiders had to wake from sleep. The female Clan member who had attacked the Leader lunged at him again. His height and long arms gave him the advantage this time, and he managed to thrust his hand spear in her shoulder.

"The Leader was probably surprised, because she did not cry out. Instead she immediately changed her weapon to the other hand and lunged at him again. This time they both fell to the ground, where she wrestled him and managed to roll on top of him. It took all of his strength to pry her arm away from his body, as he watched her spear-point closing in on his throat.

"In his whole life the Leader had never seen a female fight like this one, and her strength and courage apparently surprised him. He took hold of her good her arm with the spear and managed to twist it away from him. She was grunting like an animal, and in the darkness he would only have seen cold determination in her eyes. It was then he saw she had a sharp flint in the hand of her wounded arm, and she was trying to reach his throat to cut it. He hit her hard over the head with his spear end, and she was dazed with the knock. He rolled her from on top of him and thrust his spear into her abdomen. He knew it was a mortal blow and she would not recover from this wound.

"He shouted out to his men, 'Kill them all, even the females. The females fight just as the males do. Kill them all.' He grabbed the hand spear from the dying female's body, and with a weapon in each hand, he looked around to see whom to fight next. It was a bloody and brutal battle and even before sunrise it was all over.

"Just as Myla predicted, when the guard along the track heard the first scream from camp he went running back. He was ambushed and killed by Myla, who then hobbled down to the camp to help the Clan. Of course down there, Myla was no match for the Leader's men. So the guard was the only Outsider he managed to kill before his own death. But he would have died knowing his life had been a worthy sacrifice for his Clan.

"When it was all over, the victors were exhausted, and they sat on the ground in stunned silence. They were totally in shock at the ferocity of the fighting. It is said that the Leader had no doubts that the only reason they had been victorious was because they outnumbered their opponents. The females had fought just as strongly as his men, and it generally took two of his men to kill one of ours. He had been ever so grateful when the two sentries from the outer ridge turned up quickly.

"The Leader did a quick head count of the dead and ordered water and help for his wounded. He had lost eight of his men, and later he found the dead sentry, so this took the tally to nine of his men dead. Nearly every survivor had some sort of wound, albeit some more serious than others. They had managed to kill eight males and four females of the Wild People, with two more females wounded but not killed. He noted only one elderly male with white hair amongst the dead. So he probably realised there were a few more elderly back at the cave guarding the children, who had yet to be seen by his sentries.

"He decided to rest and feed his men before moving up to the cave. He was enraged over what had occurred, and so craved vengeance. He just wanted to see the whole thing finished. He sent two guards to bring up the prisoner.

"Poor Tula had passed an anxious night alone back at the Leader's old camp, and he had not slept at all. He was surprised when two guards returned mid light moon, but he knew straight away it was all over for his Clan. The guards looked bloodied and distant, and they treated him very roughly. By the time he reached their second camp, he was feeling very thirsty and was almost choking with the contraption around his neck.

"He noticed the Outsider's camp was in total disarray, and there was a terrible smell of blood and death everywhere. The Clan must have attacked before sunrise, which was a good strategy, but obviously it had not been successful. The first thing he noticed were the dead Clan members, whose bodies had been left where they died.

"All of the adult male hunters had been killed, as well as old Myla whom he was surprised to see there with the others. Four of the females had been killed and two other females had been wounded, one of them, Soma, having a badly injured arm. His heart skipped a beat when he could not see me, his mada. He realised I must be still up at the cave. Three of the

Leader's men were badly wounded and were receiving care. He counted nine dead Outsiders lying in a pile.

"After the Outsiders had eaten and rested, Tula was finally offered a drink of water. The Leader then spoke and the Outsiders picked up their spears. One of them was left behind to keep attending to the wounded. Tula was yanked to his feet and half dragged up the pathway towards the Clan's cave complex.

"Meanwhile, back at the Cave complex, it had been an anxious wait for me and the remaining Clan members. We could hear the commotion of the attack, the yells and screams, and then the silence. The silence was the worst part. It had been silent for some time now. So I called out to the four elderly standing behind the boulders to be ready and alert, as it looked like the Clan had been defeated."

Ula tells the listeners, "Earlier, I had put on my gazzat with knee protectors, just as I would if I were preparing to kill the Great Hairy Beast. I was still wearing the stone object around my neck. I was determined to fight to my last drop of blood to try and save the children. I hid at the entrance to the small cave, where I was able to see outside but not be seen.

"When the Leader arrived at the Cave, he got one of his men to climb a boulder, and sure enough there was one of the elderly hiding there. It was tragic, as the boulder seemed to offer no protection, and the elderly Clan member was quickly killed with the throwing spear. This process was repeated until the others were also killed. I knew then I could possibly be the last surviving Clan adult.

"The Leader then moved towards the entrance of the cave. He ordered that Tula be brought in front of him, and Tula was thrown to the ground. Tula later told me that as the cave was so quiet, he felt a flicker of hope, that perhaps I had escaped with the children much earlier, and may be hiding some distance away. But then with despair, he recognised my familiar scent. Back in the shadows of the entrance to the little cave, I was watching attentively all that was happening outside.

"I remember all my different feelings when I first saw Tula, and a cry was trapped in my throat when I realised it really was my son lying on the ground. I could hardly believe he was still alive. I could see he was tied up with a strange contraption around his neck. I told the children, 'Do not to be afraid. I am going out to help Tula.' I had a hand spear in each hand, and with arms high, I moved out of the shadows.

"As I moved into the sunlight, I momentarily looked down at Tula, and my eyes locked with his. I felt so much gratitude to know he was still alive. An Outsider raised his throwing spear, but the Leader shouted out a special command. I did not know it, but the Leader had spotted the Mother Goddess around my neck. He was shocked and confused by this."

Tula's Chant Telling of the Appearance of the Mother Goddess
It is as though time is suspended
I am lying on the ground
Watching my mada walk out of the shadows.
She is wearing her gazzat and knee protectors
And looks defiant and magnificent.
I notice the stone object around her neck
Which bobs up and down against her bosom
While she moves swiftly.
We lock eyes for an instant and
Her love travels across the void
And fills my heart,
Then she looks at the Leader.

The Leader has shouted out
So I turn my gaze to look at him.
So many expressions pass
Across the Leader's face.
Confusion, shock, amazement,
Then a look of recognition.
The Leader's eyes are locked on the stone object
Dangling around my mada's neck.
Then I see that special look
I have seen before.
It is the look of rapture,
And I understand all.

I now see my mada
Through the Leader's eyes.
The pale, white skin
Just like the stone object,
The ample bosom
And muscled thighs.
The solid stance and proud countenance
That emanates power.

Yes, the Leader really believes she is
The Mother Goddess
Here in person, before us.
I can hardly believe my own eyes.

"The Leader stepped forward towards me, and laid down his weapons on the ground. Although at the time I was unaware, it was not really me he was seeing, rather it was the Mother Goddess. I instinctively put down my weapons also. I then ran over to Tula, and I caressed his forehead.

"I think the Leader must have then realised I was Tula's mada, as he probably noticed we had the same red hair. He ordered one of his men to cut Tula's restraints and remove the strange contraption around his neck. Then he offered Tula and me some water. After drinking some water I stood up and moved towards the cave entrance and called the children to come outside. They were very frightened and unsure of the situation, but the Leader immediately offered them a water container, and they drank thirstily.

"The Leader then called out a command to his men, and they all put down their weapons. Tula then said to me and the children, 'We will be safe now.'

"When the Leader moved away to explore the cave complex, I urgently asked Tula, 'Tell me: what has happened to the Clan?'

"Tula quickly answered, 'They all are dead now, apart from the two of us and the children, and Soma and Ola, who are both wounded.' My eyes completely filled with tears.

"Tula then said with great urgency, 'Mada, please listen carefully. It is very important you know that the Leader has a strange love for the stone object hanging round your neck, that the Outsiders call the Mother Goddess. The Outsiders believe the Mother Goddess has secret powers.'

"He explained that when the Leader saw me wearing the Mother Goddess statue around my neck, he then seemed to be convinced that I was either the Mother Goddess herself, or somehow connected to her. In a raised voice, Tula quickly warned me and the children, 'You must never tell the Outsiders where we obtained Ula's Mother Goddess statue. Our lives depend on them never knowing this.'

"Inside the cave complex, the Leader once again appeared to be surprised by these strange people. The area was very well organised and comfortable, probably more so than his own dwellings back in his village. It had a very good natural structure and was much bigger than the other caves down near the river that they had searched earlier. That was probably the reason we had chosen this cave.

"The Leader stopped and inspected our tools, and again looked surprised that they were very like the tools of his own people. There were some hand spears made of a different flint that looked particularly strong. He twisted one of these and tried to bend it in his hands, but it remained intact. He examined one of the gazzats piled in the corner, and noticed the neat stitching and interesting construction. He smiled as if thinking how striking the real 'Mother Goddess' looked in hers, although I noticed he looked curiously at the knee protectors I was wearing.

"When he left the cave, Tula approached him. Once again these strange people surprised the Leader, as Tula was pointing to the children and speaking words from the Leader's own language such as 'water' and 'food'. The Leader had obviously thought we were dimwitted, but Tula had managed to somehow learn some of his language already.

"He ordered his men to go back to the temporary camp and bring up supplies for us all. Tula had managed to make it obvious that he and the Mother Goddess wanted the two wounded Clan females brought back to the cave. So the Leader ordered they be brought back as well as his own wounded. The Leader could see that the 'Mother Goddess' had spoken to her son, who was making it clear that she would take responsibility for the wounded."

Ula stops talking to the Clan members, and has a few sips of water. She needs to gather up some energy in preparation for the rest of the story. She is feeling tired just thinking about the exhausting work caring for the wounded. She says, "Tula and I both set about lighting the large fire hearth, and I hurried off but reappeared a short time later with a basket of herbs and plants. When the wounded arrived at the cave, I started cleaning the wounds, which I dabbed or washed in lotions made from boiling different plant material. Attending to my own Clan's females first, I neatly sewed the skin and tissue of the wounds together. I gave all the wounded a special bark to chew on, as this helped to ease their pain.

"It was a long dark moon time for both Tula and me as we attended to the wounded. During this time, one of the wounded Outsiders passed away. As I mentioned before, one of our Clan's females, Soma, had a terrible wound on her arm. The bottom half of her arm was dangling just near the elbow. I had seen this sort of wound before, after the hunt of the Great Hairy Beast, and I knew the bottom part of the arm needed to be cut off clean, and treated with hot stones or coals. If this was not done, the person usually became sick with a hot body before dying in great pain a few moons later.

"Although I had helped out once before with such a wound, I had never

60

actually had to do it by myself. Tula could see I looked quite anxious about it, but we both understood it had to be done. When the time came to cut away the arm, I was aware that the Leader was watching. In fact I noticed he even needed to look away while the first desperate cut was made.

"Soma understood it had to be done to save her life, and she had incredible courage. She did not cry out, not even once. Just before the flint cut through her flesh, she even looked up to me with trusting eyes, offering me a faint smile of support."

Ula becomes aware someone is sobbing, and she looks across the cave and sees it is Fasoma. Some Clan members rush over to Fasoma and touch her arm and pat her head, saying, "Soma had so much courage."

"Yes," says Fasoma, "I am sorry for interrupting your story, Ula, but I just felt so upset hearing about my mada. She really did have so much courage. And so did you, Ula, so did you. You saved my mada's life."

All the Clan members join in together. *"Ula and Soma had so much courage. Ula and Soma had so much courage."*

All the Clan members are sobbing and wailing now, totally overcome by emotion. Although in the past they have heard fragments of the story, this is the first time they have heard the full story. Ula can see they feel overwhelmed after hearing about so much courage from all of those earlier Clan members. She sits silently, allowing everyone the chance to grieve. Strangely, she has no tears herself at this moment, probably because she has already shed so many in the past. A little later, Fasoma says to her, "Ula, I am feeling better now. You can continue on with the story again."

Ula looks across to Fasoma, hesitating, "I think now is probably a good time to try and answer the earlier question of why the Clan does not have a chant about the fight. Well now you can see that neither Tula nor I were actually present at the fight, and so I have had to piece together different parts of the story as remembered and told by different people. It is like making a gazzat, where you have to sew together different pieces of the hide to make a new thing. It seems I am the only one left now, who has been able to gather up those pieces.

"As you can understand, the fight nearly destroyed the whole Clan. It killed all the adults except myself, Tula, Ola and Soma, and Soma was left with such an awful injury. The children survived, but most lost their madas and fadas, so this has affected their lives. And we all know how much Fasoma has missed not having a mada.

"After the fight, our whole way of life changed when those who survived had to live with the Outsiders. I can look back now and see how much

61

grief I suffered after the fight, especially to see so many lives wasted for no reason. I can see how incredibly busy and exhausted I became looking after the wounded, and helping all the Clan survivors. It was also confusing to live as a 'Mother Goddess'. It was a lot to go through. Such things are very hard to understand unless you have experienced them yourselves.

"So looking back now, I can say with great truth that I was just overwhelmed with what I had to deal with. I was much too exhausted to think of making a chant. Later, I tried to forget this painful time and so have locked away these memories. But now I am feeling very pleased you have heard my story this moon. As for a chant, I am too old and tired to do that. Perhaps after hearing this story someone else can make the chant, perhaps even Fasoma might do that now."

All eyes turn to Fasoma. She does not offer a yes, but she does not say no. She does hold Ula's gaze, so Ula is thinking that could mean a yes. Perhaps it will be done in the future, after Ula herself has died, and after Fasoma has had the baba. Both events will come close together, and it will not be too long now. So Ula smiles sweetly, saying, "Maybe I shall say one more thing and then we can all go to sleep.

"Just before all the Clan members started sobbing, I was talking about cutting into Soma's arm, and how I noticed the Leader had turned away. Well it appears that while looking away, the Leader was not simply being a coward, but was in fact thinking how once again our Clan members had surprised him. He was truly amazed when Soma had not screamed out in pain. In fact she had not even made a whimper. You see, even he thought we had a lot of courage.

"The Leader later told Tula that when he and his men had first arrived at the cave, he was feeling pure fury with the Wild People. This was because he had lost so many of his men in that quick and ferocious fight. It had also been particularly humiliating having to fight females, something he had never heard of before. It had left him feeling all he really wanted was vengeance. In fact he had decided then to kill us all, even the children. Of course, everything changed as soon as he saw the Mother Goddess.

"He then could understand why the fight had been so ferocious. What else could one expect when one did battle with someone like the Mother Goddess? Of course she would have some very special powers. In fact he now even considered himself very lucky to be alive at all. How fortunate he had just become a Shaman and had chosen to wear her symbol on the very day of battle. He believed this had probably saved his life.

"Later the Leader managed to convince his men how lucky they were to have been spared by the Mother Goddess. He told them they needed to be particularly respectful to her, and her son, who was called Tula, and whom she was obviously devoted to.

"Strangely the Leader saw himself and the Mother Goddess as equals, although he would always see himself as the Leader. However, for him it was still hard to understand the connection between this group of people, living so far away from his village, and his own people back home. The Shaman had never tried to explain how he discovered the Mother Goddess in the first place. Nor had the Shaman ever mentioned the Mother Goddess having a son.

"Did this mean her son would have special powers too? Perhaps the Leader thought Tula had some of her special powers, and that is why he seemed to be learning their language so magically. The Leader would have given anything to have the opportunity to ask the Shaman more about the Mother Goddess. There were just so many questions already racing around in his mind."

8

The Leader Approaches Ula

A couple of moons later, Ula tells Fasoma to come close and sit down on a hide beside her. "I would like to tell you some more of the story, Fasoma," says Ula, "but this time I would prefer to speak privately, and not in front of the younger Clan members."

"Of course, Ula," says Fasoma, wondering what was so concerning that it had to be spoken privately.

Ula begins, "Continuing on from after I had cut off Soma's dangling arm, well I did not sleep the next moon until I could see she was recovering, and was opening her eyes and looking around. I was so relieved when Soma was able to have her first drink of water. After the whole ordeal, I was just so exhausted that I fell asleep on a hide beside her. As soon as I woke up I checked on Soma, who so far was not showing any signs of the rising body temperature. I then checked on the children.

"After that, my next concern was to find out what had happened to the dead Clan members. I was very distressed when Tula told me that the Leader had all the dead, both Outsiders and Clan members, tossed out the opening at the back of the cave. I was shocked to think that's what the Outsiders would do with their dead, just leave them abandoned to the weather and scavengers. I hated to think of my Clan members lying like that at the bottom of the cliff, but there was no chance of retrieval and burial now. So I spoke to Tula and said that we must hold a Chanting Ceremony for the dead that moon, in order to honour their lives and contributions to the Clan.

"I was still very much struggling to understand myself as a Mother Goddess to the Outsiders, and so I said to Tula, 'I do not know how long I will be able to keep up the pretence of being something I clearly do not understand at all.'

"Tula explained, 'It is vital, Mada, that the Outsiders continue to think that you really are the Mother Goddess, as the Clan's lives probably depend on this belief. Mada, the best thing for you to do is to continue to wear the statue around your neck at all times, and to leave the talking between the Clan and the Outsiders up to me.'

"It was clear to me that none of the Outsiders appeared to have much interest in trying to learn the Clan's language or understand our way of life, so I could see that much was going to depend on Tula's ability to talk to them. I was greatly surprised myself that Tula was managing this new situation so well, and it showed a side of him I would never have otherwise seen in different circumstances. He had handled all of this remarkably well for someone so young. Toma would have been very impressed, not only with his ability to learn the new language but also with his strength and calmness.

"For the next several moons, I was so busy looking after the wounded and the children that I could think of little else. The Leader sent his men out to do the hunting while the older Clan children were sent out to fetch the water and firewood. The Leader seemed to expect me to cook the dark moon meal, but Tula often helped out with this task.

"One moon I complained to Tula about how lazy the Leader's men were. Tula explained to me, 'While I was held a prisoner, I noticed how the Outsiders have a different way of doing their work from us. It seems that the same person is given the same task to do every moon, so some males are always sent out hunting, others attend the fire, some just act as guards. Their system works quite well, Mada, but I think the repetition must be boring for them. It also runs the risk that, over time, the males will lose their skills in the other tasks they don't perform.'

"After the dark moon meal, the Outsiders liked to meet around the fire hearth, and do their strange chanting and movements. I found it hard to sleep with so much noise, so I decided to go into the little cave and sleep there with the younger children. I had also noticed the way the Leader watched me, and I knew it was only a matter of time before he would approach me. So one moon I decided to talk about this with Tula, and see what he thought I should do if the Leader made an approach. The very thought of an encounter made me feel quite sick and anxious. So I tried to avoid the Leader as much as possible, but this really was difficult.

"By the time two full hands of moons had passed since the day of the fighting, life seemed to have finally settled into a routine, and all the wounded were recovering well. However, both Tula and I were very upset that we would miss the annual hunt of the Great Hairy Beast. Tula attempted to talk to the Leader about this matter. He took some hide of the animal and made an outline in the dirt of the Great Hairy Beast and some hunters standing around it with raised spears. Just like Tula the first time he saw the Leader make the markings in the dirt, I was quite intrigued with this and, like Tula, thought the story in the dirt was a very clever idea.

"The Leader understood what Tula was trying to tell him, but he just had no interest in the hunt of such a large and dangerous-looking animal. Besides, why bother as there appeared to be plenty of animals with soft eyes and other animals readily available. He just waved his hands and said 'no' and became very irritated when Tula brought up the matter again two moons later. However, Tula stood his ground and decided to go off and see if he could locate the herd."

Ula lowers her voice now, and her eyes look around the cave to make sure no one is close enough to listen in. Fasoma leans in a little closer. "One moon, while Tula was away, I went down to the river area with Suta and two of the younger children to collect some special herbs and plants. I had by now used up all my supplies of plant remedies. We were closely examining how to collect some special resin from one of the trees, when a shadow moved across the grass.

"I looked up and saw the Leader standing there, and he was staring at me in a peculiar way. I was surprised because I had not heard his approach, being so involved talking to the children. He signalled with a casual movement of his arm for Suta and the younger children to return to the camp, and when I turned to leave also, he took my arm firmly.

"I was so shocked and flustered, as I realised what was about to happen. I had expected the approach, should it occur, would probably take place outside the little cave where I slept at night. I always imagined the Leader would speak to Tula first, who would then seek my approval for such a partnership. This is the way the Clan members always go about this matter. I was not expecting this. I could feel my face redden, and my heart started beating strongly.

"I did have an urge to scream and run away, but I remembered my talk with Tula, which ended with him saying, 'It would be better to accept his attentions and not to resist when the time comes.' I was thinking of those words as the Leader pulled me down onto the grass under the tree, where he treated me firmly but not roughly.

"It is hard to describe my feelings as I lay there, but I did not want to look at him, nor did I close my eyes. Instead I turned my head away and examined how the shadows and sunlight flickered together on the grass, looking almost as though they were playing with each other. I could hear the breeze whispering in the branches above, and so barely noticed the throaty, rutting noises the Leader was making. Surprisingly the whole episode was over very quickly, so strong was his urgency after so long without a female.

"As we walked back to the cave complex, I knew I would have to be careful to hide my true feelings from him. Tula had said a number of times that the lives of our Clan members probably depended on my having a successful relationship with the Leader. That kept going through my thoughts, over and over. I was still feeling so flustered I forgot the container of herbs, which was still under the tree, and so on the way back I realised I would have to return for them the next moon. The Leader did not say a word to me during the walk back, but kept taking secret glances at me, which I pretended not to notice. That dark moon I simply told the children to leave the little cave as the Leader would be sleeping there now."

Fasoma sees tears pouring down Ula's face, as Ula looks increasingly distressed. "I just felt so ashamed, Fasoma," Ula says, "so ashamed. Never have I heard of a Clan female being treated like this."

Fasoma puts her arms around Ula and sobs quietly with her. "You should never have felt ashamed, Ula." Fasoma sobs. "It was the Leader and not you who did the wrong thing."

After the sobbing has finished, Ula looks up at Fasoma and says, "I have never had the courage to tell anyone about this, until now. I did not even tell Tula, as I knew how much he would have been upset. Sometimes I think Suta may have known, as when I returned with the Leader, she looked at me strangely and kept asking, 'Are you all right, Ula? Are you sure you are all right?'

"The dark moon after the approach, when the Leader moved into the little cave to sleep with me, one of his men talked to the Leader asking permission to take Soma for his partner. This man of course was Faru, your fada. He had taken an interest in Soma who was making a good recovery from her dreadful arm injury. The Leader considered Faru's request and gave his consent. I saw Faru approach Soma outside the cave. It was quite moving to watch, as he took hold of her good hand and, with hands locked together, pointed to her and then pointed to his chest, with such a loving look in his eyes. Soma smiled and kept saying, 'Meta meta,' and hugged him tightly."

Now it is Fasoma's turn to sob quietly, but this time the tears are happy ones. It is the first time she has heard this story, and it is good to hear her mada had been so pleased about this partnership. Ula continues, "So the next dark moon, Faru set up a hide tent for his new sleeping quarters. It was clear to me that Soma was actually quite relieved about it. She said to me, 'Ula, I am thankful to have the interest of a male to help me, especially now, as I have only the use of one good arm. Besides, I was so worried the Head Scout might take an interest in me. Also, I do think this Outsider seems very kind.' However, we were both very concerned about what was going to happen to poor Ola now, and the girls too, especially Suta when she matured more.

"I remember Tula looking quite surprised when he returned to find that such a big change in sleeping arrangements had occurred in such a short time. However, as the camp seemed quite settled, he just accepted the new arrangements. Although I suspected he must have been secretly pleased to be away at that time. He never asked me about the matter so I never spoke about it to him. But I will tell you now, there has hardly been a moon since when I have not thought about that moon and what happened under the tree. It is like one of those stories you see in the dirt, only instead I see it in my thoughts. Unfortunately, I keep seeing it all the time."

9

Faru Talks to the Clan Members

It is important to face the truth,
We use the truth to move forward.

Fasoma can see there is a growing interest amongst the Clan members about Ula's stories, and much anticipation about when they can all sit down again and listen. Faru tells Fasoma that he would like to talk to the Clan members, and so asks for permission to speak the next moon. Fasoma says to him, "As Ula is the main storyteller, I shall check with her, but I think she will be pleased to have you speak."

* * *

When Fasoma speaks to Ula, Ula quickly realises there is a problem. "But Faru does not speak the Clan's language," says Ula, "and Suta and I do not speak the Outsiders' language."

Fasoma gently slaps her own face. "Of course you are right, Ula, but perhaps I can take Tula's role as interpreter on this occasion." Ula nods and smiles gently, as any comment about Tula pleases her greatly. So after the next main meal, Fasoma gathers all the Clan members around the fireplace to listen to the story as told by Faru and then retold by Fasoma.

Faru begins, "The Leader and I grew up together as best friends back in our village, and had been inseparable from childhood. Our madas were sistas, so we had a blood tie as well. I had always greatly admired and loved the Leader." The fact they come from the same family is of great interest to the Clan members, for no one had been aware of this before. Ula quietly thinks to herself how different the two males were, which made it even harder to believe they came from the same family. But that now explained

Faru's great loyalty to the Leader, which was clearly seen and known by all.

Faru continues, "I was the one who had more contact with the Clan than any of the Leader's other males. Firstly I was with the scouting party when we came across Toma, whom we later ambushed before the Head Scout speared and killed him. At the time I did not think we should have killed him, but the Head Scout was in charge, so it was his decision. I will admit that I too had thought Toma was cowardly and stupid. Of course I later realised this could not have been further from the truth, and I am greatly sorry about this mistake. The regret of his death has lived with me ever since." While it is still quite painful for both Ula and Fasoma to listen to this part of the story, neither has ever blamed Faru for Toma's death.

"Just like the Leader, during the great fight between the two peoples, I had been totally amazed with the Clan members' fighting skills, especially those of the females. I had never seen a female warrior before. Back in my village, the females were certainly not trained or allowed to take part in fighting. This was strictly for males. I have never told anyone this before, but I was the person who wounded Soma, but I knew she never realised this, and I never told her."

Everyone turns now to look at Fasoma, whose face has turned pale, but is not betraying her feelings. "I am deeply ashamed that I wounded your mada," says Faru. "And, Fasoma, I hope you can forgive me for telling you this now for the first time."

Fasoma says, "*It is important to face the truth.*"

And all the Clan members repeat, "*It is important to face the truth.*"

"*We use the truth to move forward,*" says Fasoma.

"*We use the truth to move forward,*" repeat the Clan members. Fasoma looks up and smiles at her fada. It is a sweet smile, thinks Ula, definitely a smile of forgiveness.

"After the great fight, I was the person who assisted Ula with the surgery on Soma's arm. It was the most gruesome thing I had ever done, but it left me in awe of the great courage displayed by both Ula and Soma. When the half limb was amputated, Soma did not make a sound, but grimaced and bit down hard on a piece of hide. Compared to Soma, the Leader's males who were wounded acted like whimpering children, moaning and screaming out whenever their wounds were touched."

"*Ula and Soma had so much courage. Ula and Soma had so much courage,*" say all the Clan members.

"It was Soma's welfare that led to my staying around at the cave complex each moon," says Faru. "I wanted to help with Soma's recovery, such was my guilt even then. I just wanted to see her get better. When I attended to her, she would look softly into my eyes and with genuine gratitude, say 'meta', which at the time I understood to mean thank you. It was after half a moon cycle, when she was out of danger and recovering well, that she gave me her first smile. With it she looked deeply into my eyes and held my gaze.

"No one had ever looked into my eyes like that before, and I felt something touched us both. I was surprised that this had happened, but realised straight away I had special feelings for her and wanted her as a partner. I also realised I needed to claim her quickly before one of the other men did. I was especially concerned about the Head Scout, and so I spoke to the Leader about her." All the Clan members are smiling now, especially Fasoma, as they enjoy hearing about this great love story, as Faru has always called it, between a Clan member and an Outsider.

Faru continues, "I was content spending most of my time at the cave complex, happily helping Ula and Tula with chores such as cooking, bringing up water from the river, keeping the fire going, and looking after the wounded. The Leader's other men were only interested in going hunting for food, and then coming back to the cave and sitting around. So it was left to me and the small group of Clan survivors to do the rest of the work. The first half a moon cycle was an incredibly busy and difficult time for Ula, who had taken charge of attending to all the wounded. I could see she was exhausted.

"Once I went out with Tula, and I saw the herd of the Great Hairy Beast, or mammoths as I named them, after the word which in my language means 'huge'. They were certainly an amazing sight to see, but I just could not imagine how the Clan members were able to kill one of these huge animals. Again, it made me realise what great courage the Clan members must possess to do this every full season, putting their lives at such risk each time. I remember asking Tula, 'How do your people manage to kill such a large animal with just a hand spear?'

"Tula patiently explained, and in great detail as Tula always did. Even if you asked him just a simple question, his answer seemed to go on forever. He said, 'Of course the Clan needs very strong hand spears to hunt the Great Hairy Beast and other large animals, which all have very tough hides that have to be penetrated by the hand spear. Our strong spears help us a great deal, and our chanting history tells us that long ago some other clans developed a way of making these.

"This special hand spear is carefully made by first selecting an especially strong flint stone, gathered from far away. This is sharpened and bound to a wooden shaft, and then the flint head is glued to the shaft with a sticky black glue. This black glue is a Clan-made pitch, made from heating birch bark to a very high temperature, by a special heating method. This makes the hand spear very strong. The flint stone will not break off when we thrust into the thick animal hide.'

"Tula went on further to say, 'The black glue is very useful and sometimes we also use it to attach a hide or the stomach of a large animal, as a lining to an animal skull. We place this on top of a stone hearth with a wood fire lit below, or else we place it on a pile of heated stones, often to simmer *soupa* or stews. One moon I will give you a lesson, Faru, on how to make the black glue. I warn you though it takes a lot of effort and practice to do it properly.'

"It was easy to see how proud Tula always seemed about his Clan and how eager he was to explain their way of life," says Faru. "He loved talking about the Clan, and once he explained to me, 'It is part of our way of living that all possessions and food are shared equally among the Clan members, and all members contribute to and share equally all duties. Unlike your people, Faru, both males and females are expected to take on the duties of hunting, gathering, tool making, cooking, hide preparations, training the children, and attending to the fire and the woodpile. The only exception we make is that females are not expected to hunt large animals when pregnant or breastfeeding, nor are the elderly Clan members expected to hunt large animals.'

"One moon, when discussing my loving partnership with Soma, Tula went on to explain, 'In our Clan, a male and female mate for life. If one Clan member wants a partnership, or if the Clan members decide there should be a partnership, then the Clan will hold a meeting to discuss the matter. If the partnership is approved at the meeting, then each of two must give their permission for this partnership. Also, there is usually no partnership allowed between close members such as mada and fada and their own children, or between a brada and sista.

"'If there is an unequal number of Clan members, then the odd member is allowed to share a mate of his or her choosing, as long as that Clan member consents. Every generation or so, a Clan may meet up with another Clan, usually during the annual hunt of the Great Hairy Beast. This may be the only time when one Clan actually gets to see another Clan, and it provides an opportunity for an exchange of Clan members, something that is helpful to both the clans. We also always very closely watch the way animal families breed so that we understand their ways too.'

"I must admit," says Faru, "That I found myself admiring the way the Clan members lived their lives in such a simple and honest fashion. I particularly found Tula such a joy, and I liked his honesty and openness. Tula was always so enthusiastic about sharing information, such as how to make the black glue. Already I had more companionship with him than any of the Leader's men. He was really like a brada to me." All the Clan members now turn to look at Ula, who is smiling and nodding her head with approval. Everyone loved Tula, and Ula is always happy when someone says kind words about him.

Faru continues, "It was obvious to me that Tula seemed to have no feelings of hate or vengeance towards the Leader or his men, and I could plainly see what peaceful people the Clan members really were. And so I have always believed the Clan members would never have attacked the Leader's men if you had been left alone. I have felt great guilt about the Leader's actions, and have thought it was a bad misjudgement of the Leader, to plan to attack. The result of this decision has led to so many of both peoples being killed.

"Before the Leader's arrival, I can see that the Clan would have lived a quiet and ordered life. After the great fight, it was obvious that Ula was then trying to restore a sense of this former calmness to the children, and re-establish a sense of routine and purpose back into their lives. Truly, Ula worked very hard to get things back to normal and the Clan should be very grateful to her." All the Clan members smile and look at Ula, who is smiling too, as she has enjoyed this praise from Faru. Ula knows the Clan members are grateful, and so there is no need of praise from them.

Faru says, "It is interesting that before I lived with the Clan, I had never had any interest in children. I was amazed when I found I was greatly enjoying the Clan children. Most of them had lost their mada and fada, and so seemed to appreciate any show of warmth. I enjoyed teaching some of them how to throw a spear, and had agreed with Tula to take them out on a hunting party as soon as the weather warmed. Sometimes I forgot to include the female children in the lesson, but they quietly stepped forward, even the smallest of them, to remind me they were to have the lessons as well as the male children.

"I noticed that Tula was managing to learn our language very quickly, and I could not understand how he was doing this. While both the Leader and I struggled trying to learn enough words to communicate with the Clan, Tula only had to hear one of our words once to remember it. I believed Tula would be fluent with my language by the end of the cold season, a truly amazing achievement. I do think the Leader believed Tula had some magical qualities, but I did not believe that. It almost seemed silly that the Leader's men still referred to the Clan members as the Wild People, when I could see nothing wild or backward about you. In fact I thought my own people had a great deal to learn from you.

"I noticed your Clan members were very skilled at making tools. I was particularly impressed with a very useful tool that you called a *lizzwa*, and which you made from the ribs of the red animal with soft eyes. This tool was used to make the animal hides smooth and shiny, and most importantly to stop water passing through the hide. The tool was made in a clever way because although it looked like a very simple tool, it managed to use the special features of the animal's bone, both its toughness as well as its flexibility, as you pressed it against the hide.

"In your tool collection you had sewing tools carved out of bone, and these were used to sew animal hides together, to make clothing, tents and other useful things. Tools such as hand axes, hand spears and flints were stored in the branch of the cave with the smaller fire hearth. Because the cave complex was so far from the river, you also stored water in large hide containers, again made out of the treated hides stretched over a framework of animal bones that were tied together. You carefully made your stone flints, usually sitting outside the cave area, to keep the inside free of debris, only working inside during poor weather.

"Most interesting was the way the Clan members made some items, when you tended to use your teeth and mouth a bit like a third hand. I watched you hold animal hides and tools with your teeth, while using your hands for cutting or sewing. I found it quite interesting to watch this, especially when you tried to talk at the same time." All the Clan members chuckle here, as they know exactly what Faru is talking about. Faru continues, "Tula told me that this practice of using your teeth for sewing tended to wear down your teeth, although he claimed your teeth were actually quite strong.

"Quite often I noticed you picked things up from the ground using your toes instead of your hands. At first I thought you were just too lazy to bend down, but then I realised you could pick something up much more quickly this way. So now I have started doing that too.

"I also found it interesting how you used hot stones and oils extracted from a special plant to give each other massages, to help with sore joints and muscle pain. Although it was harder for Soma to give me a massage with only one good arm, she still managed it." Again the Clan members chuckle, before Faru continues, "I was very impressed that both adults and children were experts in preparing splints and slings for broken limbs, as broken limbs and sprains were quite common, especially when hunting the larger animals.

"I can remember one moon while sitting down resting after chopping up a lot of firewood, that I silently compared your skills with those of my people. When it came to tool making and weapon making, we were practically the same, except my people had the throwing spear, while the Clan had the strong black glue to attach the spearhead. I did think that your knowledge about healing and plant remedies was much greater than ours.

"In my village back home, only the Shaman practised healing. So many of the villagers actually missed out on real help, particularly if the Shaman was busy. Whereas all of the Clan members gained the knowledge of healing herbs and how to attend to broken bones and stitch up wounds." Here Faru stops and shakes his head and smiles to himself. "At times there must have been some terrible wounds to attend to, especially after the hunt of the mammoth. So having only one person with such knowledge of remedies and healing would have been foolish for the Clan.

"But even more than your courage and commonsense," Faru says, "It has been your complete closeness as a group that has shown the best about you. There was no ranking of one above the other, no jealousy or rivalry between you. Everyone was equal and you all worked together with a sense of purpose, always in the best interests of the Clan. I really found this way of life to be truly amazing and quite inspiring. However, neither the Leader nor any of the other men seemed to be aware of these obvious and impressive qualities of the Clan, so really I was left to think about these matters alone."

All the Clan members are sitting very quietly while listening to Faru's words. Ula is thinking that it is interesting how someone from outside the Clan views the Clan members and their way of life with such different eyes. What the Clan members see as normal and ordinary, an Outsider sees as different and sometimes extraordinary. Perhaps it is a good thing if you can sometimes view yourself as if through another's eyes. Perhaps then you can see even more about yourself. "*We need to keep our eyes open to really see ourselves,*" says Ula.

Faru has more to say. "Since I started living with the Clan, I realised that I was changing and becoming a different person. I was quickly growing tired of the Leader's ceremonies with their frenzied singing and dancing. I much preferred to sit in on the Clan's chanting sessions, where I found your deep, hushed voices more soothing to my spirit, even if I could not understand your words.

"I did have some concern about the Leader, as I also felt he had changed since his encounter with the Clan. Though it was hard to work out exactly what that change was. To me the Leader seemed a little lost, and was sometimes not in complete control as he had always been before. It was also apparent to me that the Leader seemed to have lost the respect of some of the men, something that he always had in abundance before we had contact with the Clan.

"To be honest I never felt comfortable that the Leader had also taken on the role of Shaman, and thought it would have been better if he had just stayed as the Leader. However, because of my great loyalty to him, I never admitted these thoughts to anyone, especially not the Leader himself. I decided to keep a close eye on the other men to make sure there was no trouble brewing with any of the men, particularly the Head Scout. He always looked so surly and unhappy."

Faru is looking a little hesitant when he starts talking again. "There was another matter that could not escape my attention. There was a part of me that had never quite accepted that Ula was indeed the real Mother Goddess." Ula's head jerks up now. Faru has mentioned her name and the Mother Goddess. "However," says Faru, "No matter how hard I tried, I was at a loss to explain how Ula was wearing one of our statues around her neck, on the moon of the great fight. I had spoken to Tula about the matter on a number of occasions, but Tula always just grunted and shrugged and never gave an answer.

"It was after about two to three moon cycles had passed since the great fight with the Clan that everyone was complaining about the cold. Tula assured me, 'This cold season is unusually cold, and we have never had so much snow before. It snows nearly every moon now.' We could both see that the Leader's men were not happy. They had never experienced such cold weather. In fact it was the first time they had ever seen snow. Several of the men had said they wanted to camp down near the river where the icy conditions did not seem to be so severe."

Ula, who has been listening carefully, suddenly interrupts Faru as she has something to add to this part of the story. "Yes, I had been thinking hard how to help protect the hunters, who complained so much about the cold. This led me to come up with a new idea, where I mixed some fire ash into some fat, and made a thick paste. On the really cold moons when the hunters needed to leave the cave, they put this paste all over their arms and faces to help protect their skin from the biting cold. It seemed to work quite well, although the Head Scout did not like to spread it on his body. He complained it was too greasy and smelly for his skin.

"In order to further help the hunters endure the icy weather conditions, I also came up with another good idea. This idea was to use some of the dead Clan members' gazzats to make leggings to help keep the hunters warm when they went out hunting. I recut some of the gazzats into long continuous strips, and the hunters wound these strips around their feet and legs, and wore them under their hides for extra warmth. I also used some knee pads to make some special coverings for their feet, and I placed grooves in the underneath section, so they would not slip on the icy rocks."

The Clan members all congratulate Ula on her good ideas, as the leggings are still used at this time. Fasoma also comments, "I think Tula got his inventive thoughts from you, Ula, for really you also had some very useful ideas to improve the life of the Clan members."

Faru is becoming a little annoyed with the interruptions from others. "There are too many storytellers now," says Faru. "I am nearly done so let me finish now.

"I wanted to tell you how Tula and the other Clan survivors were greatly saddened that the herd of the mammoths had long departed, making this the first cold season when the Clan had not held a hunt. Indeed, Tula had really tried hard to make the Leader understand the importance of the hunt. Twice he had gone out looking for the herd, and the second time he had even taken me with him. Tula enjoyed seeing my amazement when I first saw the mammoths. But really I just considered it was too dangerous to hunt such a large animal.

"Although there were still plenty of the animal with soft eyes, and other animals around, Tula explained that these animals did not provide the Clan with the bone marrow that was so nutritious for them, and even more importantly the great layers of fat. He said the fat had so many uses that the Clan members were not sure if they would be able to manage without it. As Ula has since told me, 'We add the fat to the meat when cooking, to improve the flavour. As well, before a very strenuous activity we sometimes just eat the fat on its own, as we think that it gives us extra strength to carry on with such an activity.' "

Faru sits back now, looking very pleased with himself. Now all the other Clan members congratulate him on his very good storytelling and very clear memories. They have really enjoyed his story.

* * *

Fasoma can see it has been good for her fada to take part in the storytelling, and perhaps he could be included again in the future. She will have a talk to Ula the next moon and see what part of the story Ula thinks should be told next, and who should tell it.

10

The Head Scout

Toma helped the Clan to survive.

"The younger Clan members keep asking to hear about the Head Scout," says Fasoma to Ula.

"I don't know why," says Ula. "Nobody liked him."

"I think that's why they want to hear more about him," says Fasoma. "They are curious about him."

"Well I don't want to talk about him. Ask Faru or Suta to do this," says Ula. Later when the Clan children hear that someone will be talking about the Head Scout, there seems to be some extra chatter, and they gather around the fire hearth even earlier than usual.

Fasoma talks to Suta, and they decide that Faru is the best Clan member to talk about the Head Scout, as he is the one who really knows the most about him. Faru is very pleased to be asked to talk again. So after the main meal, when all are seated, he begins, "The Head Scout was a person with a huge presence. He was a head taller than any of the other males from our village, and he had a strong and athletic body."

Fasoma interrupts shyly, "Faru, can you place a mark on the cave wall to show us how tall he really was." Faru gathers up a piece flint and scratches a mark on the cave wall near the entrance. "Meta, Faru" says Fasoma, looking somewhat in awe, as she can now see just how tall he really was.

Ula's nose crinkles up, just as though she is sniffing the death smell. She is struggling to understand Fasoma's interest in the height of the Head Scout. But now she can see it is not only Fasoma who has an interest, it is also some of the other younger Clan members, whose eyes seemed to be locked on the flint scratching made by Faru.

"You probably don't know this," says Faru, "but the Head Scout also came from an important family back in the village. He was well respected by all the village males. Before coming away with the Leader, he held an important position and was the Head Guard to the Village Chief. He was considered to be a highly trusted and loyal guard to the Village Chief, who as you know was the Leader's fada. He was chosen by the Village Chief to accompany the Leader on both of the voyages to the distant lands, and it was his duty to guard and obey the Leader even to his own death.

"However, ever since the Leader first saw Ula, or Mother Goddess as he called her, the Head Scout felt that life seemed to have totally changed for them all. He thought the Leader seemed obsessed with the Mother Goddess, even to the extent of placing a taboo on harming her or her son. The Head Scout did not trust the boy Tula, whom he believed was the son of the Wild Person he first encountered and killed. He always believed the boy would want to seek vengeance should he discover who was responsible for his fada's death.

"I think the Head Scout really wanted to kill Tula but did not dare risk the Leader's wrath."

"See," says Ula, "I have told you he was a very bad male. Remember he was the one who brutally killed Toma for no reason at all."

"Yes, yes, Ula, you are right. We all know that," says Faru. "I remember that the Head Scout thought there was something very strange about the Wild People – as he always called the Clan members. He did not like their reactions to the worship of the Mother Goddess. He had made a point of watching them very closely during ceremonies held by the Leader. It was obvious to him that the Clan members had no interest whatsoever in the identity and worship of the Mother Goddess. Even the children showed the same marked indifference.

"In his mind he felt this indicated that there was something terribly wrong, something that just did not make sense. He did not wish to question the Leader, and was too scared to voice his concerns to the other men, lest he was punished or killed for his disloyalty to the Leader. He was always very careful what he said in front of me, as he knew I was absolutely loyal to the Leader because of our blood ties.

"But like me, he also believed the Leader had overstepped his authority when he took on the role of Shaman to the Mother Goddess. The Head Scout did not believe, as the Leader did, that Ula was the real Mother Goddess. He probably thought she was some sort of a false Mother Goddess. He thought the real Mother Goddess had been angered when the Leader took on the role of Shaman, and had sent this false Mother Goddess to punish us all. He even thought this false Mother Goddess had taken over and poisoned the Leader's mind. He was absolutely convinced that if they continued to stay in this place with the false Mother Goddess, they were all doomed to die."

Here, Ula can't resist a scoffing laugh and saying, "Now you can clearly see just how muddled were their thoughts. The whole Mother Goddess worship was a complete mystery to the Clan members. We just could not understand any of it. One moon I was Ula, and the next moon I was a Mother Goddess or a false Mother Goddess. It was very confusing."

"Yes," said Faru, "It was also hard for us to understand how this Wild Woman from so far away from our village, happened to be wearing the very same statue around her neck as one of our statues. Anyway, back to the Head Scout, who I agree was definitely the most confused of all. He knew that at some stage he had misplaced his own statue, but it did not even occur to him that the Mother Goddess's statue could actually be his lost one. However, he was certain he could never voice any dangerous doubts about the Mother Goddess to others.

"Also, the Head Scout became very frustrated about living in the cave complex. He could not see the sense of living up in the cave so far away from the river. It was much easier to hunt down at the river as the game was always going to the river to drink, especially to the large flat rock area. Also it seemed stupid to make constant trips to the river to bring back water to the cave. He felt these two matters outweighed the comfort of the cave complex. Certainly, as winter progressed, he found it was so much colder up on the ridges. So in his mind any advantages offered by the cave complex were then outweighed completely by the disadvantages.

"After the great fight, it was natural that the Leader would take partnership with the Mother Goddess, but he was shocked when the Leader allowed me to take partnership with Soma or, as he called her, the Wild Woman with the wounded arm. As Head Scout to the Leader, he expected that he would be offered this victory prize, not that he cared for Soma at all. It was simply his expectation because of his special position and long years of service and loyalty to the Leader and the Leader's fada.

"After this first refusal, he assumed the Leader would then give him the other female, Ola, and when he asked for her, the Leader again refused. This left him feeling angry and he was sure the Mother Goddess must somehow have been behind this last refusal.

"I must say that the Head Scout was very unhappy living with the Clan members in the cave complex. Without a doubt, he really did not like the

81

Wild People at all. He was always saying how he found them incredibly dirty and smelly. 'They never wash their bodies,' he would say. Back in our village, our people bathed every day in the ocean, and were certainly never smelly or covered in the irritating creatures that now also drove him crazy with itching all night. You see The Head Scout had always been particularly concerned about his cleanliness and appearance.

"Back home, he had a very long swim in the sea first thing each morning. Then after drying himself, he covered his body in the special oil that the females crushed out of the argan nuts growing in the area. He also cupped the oil in his hands and stroked it through his hair with his fingers, pulling his hair back behind his ears. He loved to see his dark skin shiny and glowing, and he would walk around the village looking and feeling just like a god himself.

"When we moved into the cave complex, he tried to continue some sort of a daily cleaning ritual. Each morning he heated some water in one of the black animal skulls, stripped naked before the fire, and washed his body with a piece of hide."

"I shall tell you one thing he used to do," says Ula, almost sniggering. "He loved to show off his nakedness, especially in front of the females. You see not only was he proud of being tall and strong, but he was also particularly proud of his very large male part.

"I remember one particular time after his wash that he used some of my special oils to rub his male part, right in front of poor Ola. With startled eyes, she watched it grow to an enormous size. She ran away into the small cave, truly terrified, hearing his jeering laughter following her. After that episode the Clan females always tried to leave the cave when it came to his ritual washing time.

"Unfortunately for me, one moon the Head Scout tried some of my *sopa*, and he was impressed with it. He then took to using it each moon, much to my alarm, as he was using up the only supplies the Clan had. Remember we had hardly any fat left to make more sopa. Tula had gone to the trouble of telling him, 'My mada makes the sopa by boiling wood ash and animal fat. She also boils and extracts oil from the leaves of a special plant that has a sweet smell, and adds this to the sopa mixture. The Clan uses the special sopa when they bathe to kill off the skin mites and lice.'

"The Head Scout then asked Tula, 'How often do you all bathe?'

"Tula replied, 'We usually bathe twice every full season, first just after the beginning of the warm season and then just at the end. We also wash our hides with this sopa during the warm season, and then dry these in the sunlight.' You should have seen the look of scorn on the Head Scout's face with that reply."

"It is true," says Faru. "The Head Scout was scathing about the fact that the Clan members only bathed twice a full season. He was aware the river water did not compare to the sparkling, clean waters of the sea back home. But it was with absolute contempt that he watched the Clan's children busily delousing one another around the small fire hearth. It greatly annoyed him to watch the Clan members continually scratch, and then pick at the small scabs that inevitably formed after so much scratching.

"The Head Scout spoke often about a matter that made him particularly incensed. This was that the females seemed to think they could do anything the males could do, and so the idea that they were allowed to hunt and fight was really quite shocking to him. He simply chose to ignore the fact that they could do both extremely well.

"I know he disliked the Clan's chanting ceremonies, which he thought sounded silly. He could never understand the fact that Clan members did not appear to be able to sing or dance. This convinced him that the Clan members were nothing but backward fools."

"See I told you all," says Ula, "that the Head Scout was a bad and brutal male, even his face had cruel eyes." But as she says this, Ula is noticing that the other Clan members are silent. The expression on the faces of some of her Clan members is not one of strong disapproval that she is expecting to see, but rather more of continuing curiosity. This forces her to now look at her thoughts and to try to see things differently. She is aware that of course some of the younger Clan members have never known the Head Scout, and so to them he is just a name. Ah, but a name that is very well known.

Ula feels a bit crushed as she also realises that to these Clan members, Toma is also just a name. Therefore, hearing about Toma is probably not nearly as interesting to them as hearing about the Head Scout. After all who is Toma to them? Of course they know that Toma was the first Clan member killed by the Outsiders. They also know that Toma found the statue of the Mother Goddess, but the Clan chants do not really say much more about him. Ula's grief at Toma's death has stopped her from talking about him, and she now sees that has been a mistake.

Faru continues, "The coldness of the winter was becoming unbearable, and one day when out hunting with some of the males, the Head Scout suggested to them the idea of moving down to the river. He was surprised when they instantly agreed with him. They said that they too had observed the milder climate and other advantages of being closer to the river. The fact that some of the males agreed with him emboldened him to take up the matter with the Leader.

"When he spoke to the Leader, the Leader did not object, although we all noticed the Leader's brow creased a little. The Head Scout quickly assured the Leader that his group would share their hunting kills with the others up in the cave complex. Then the Leader gave a silent approval with a nod of the head. The Head Scout couldn't leave fast enough, and so it was that the very next moon that he and four others left the cave complex with some supplies.

"Down near the big bend in the river, they set up camp in one of the caves in the limestone cliff embankments. They had not carried down any wood from the cave complex, so collecting that was one of their first tasks, as they needed to keep a fire going at all times. They had not brought any fat supplies or wild berries that the Clan members ate, although they were offered some. When they arrived at the river cave, it was so cold that most of the river seemed to be iced over, and even cutting wood was not easy, as ice covered just about everything.

"The Head Scout had never ventured far away enough to catch sight of the mammoths, although some moons earlier, I had told him all about the animals. Like the Leader, he and the other men had no interest in hunting such large prey. By this time all of them had quickly grown tired of meals that consisted mostly of meat. They were greatly missing their fresh seafood and vegetables. They were also finding that the meat was becoming harder to eat as their gums were sore and bloody now, and their teeth seemed to be almost moving in the gums as well."

"Let me talk now," says Ula, "and tell everyone the story of the sick Outsider."

"Of course, Ula, this is really your story anyway," says Faru, a little surprised that Ula has offered to talk about the Outsiders.

Ula begins, "Not long later, while living in the cave down by the river, one of the Outsiders fell ill with a high temperature. He was coughing up a thick stickiness that was stained with blood, and he was too weak to move. So the Head Scout sent one of the males up to the cave complex for some of my healing herbs.

"The Head Scout was quite surprised when I arrived some time later. I set about making a soupa with some meat of the animal with soft eyes, and I added some herbs, and thickened it with a chestnut paste. When finished I tried to give some to the sick scout, who barely managed a few small sips. I motioned to the Head Scout and others to eat the soupa. I could tell that they found it was easier to eat the meat cooked this way, as it was so much more tender and the chewing did not hurt their gums as much.

"I stayed up all night with the sick male, trying several healing steam vapours, but he died before the sunrise. After he died, the Head Scout ordered two of the males to carry the body out of the cave and leave it in the snow. It was only then that I realised that the Outsiders never buried their dead. I know he was aware that the Clan members buried our dead up in the area of the cave complex. I imagined he could not understand why we went to so much trouble, when they didn't."

Here Faru interrupts, "I think he thought that when you buried a dead body, you were just trying to cover up the smell. He often remarked how he noticed the Clan members always seemed to be sniffing the air, and so he thought you must have had sensitive noses."

"Anyway," continues Ula, "after making another batch of soupa and leaving some herbs and berries, I left to go back to the cave complex."

"I would say that it was after the death of one of his men in these wretched circumstances," says Faru, "that the Head Scout realised what a forlorn place this was. He understood how much he wished to return home to a warmer climate, and proper food and friends, especially female company, again. He must have told the others in his cave that as soon as the weather warmed he intended to return home. They would have all agreed they wanted to leave with him. I am sure that none of them believed they would manage to survive another winter. Nor did they believe the Leader would ever leave the Mother Goddess.

"The Head Scout would have warned them they must all promise to keep this decision a secret from the Leader and the others in the cave complex. Occasionally some in the cave complex came across the other men down in the valley, though we were seeing them less often now. Whenever the Clan members saw them they noticed that these men never looked very happy.

"Tula told me how he and his mada had talked about this very matter, and how they both felt sure the Head Scout and his men intended to quietly disappear back home, when the warmer weather came again. Tula was very aware that the Head Scout had hard, cruel eyes, and had noticed how he always looked at him strangely. Tula had remarked to his mada a number of times, 'I would not be surprised if he is the Outsider who killed Fada.' Although never admitting this to be the case, I had warned Tula to watch his back if he was out hunting near the Head Scout. So I know that Tula always took great care when he came across his tracks, which were easily recognisable because they were so large."

Faru looks across to Ula, "Why don't you finish the story, Ula, as I cannot think of more to say now."

"Yes," says Ula, "I think I would just like to mention Tula's ability to learn the Outsiders' language. He was progressing really well with his understanding of the language. He said how he really found their language quite interesting, because it differed in that it was really simpler. He explained how the Outsiders had just one word: 'mammoth', for the Clan's three words: 'Great Hairy Beast', and likewise their word is 'deer' for the Clan's 'animal with soft eyes'.

"It was obvious to me that the Outsiders, including the Leader, did not have any interest in trying to understand the Clan's language, and so this led to Tula adopting the role of 'interpreter' as they called it. Some of the younger children were showing some interest in trying to learn the Outsiders' language, but this worried me. I just wanted to see the children spend the time learning their own stories rather than learning the language of the Outsiders.

"I was always worried that one moon the Head Scout would turn his attentions towards Ola. She was absolutely terrified of him. She had even told me privately that she would be prepared to jump out the opening in the back of the cave, rather than live with the Head Scout down in the river cave. I felt I needed to try and protect Ola, so one moon when Tula and I were alone I whispered, 'I believe Soma is with child, but it is very early days yet. It is good news, as Soma seems quite content and her partner, Faru. He is surprisingly gentle and attentive to her. You should take up a partner, Tula. Have you thought of taking Ola as your partner? I know she is older than you, but it would be best for her to have a partner to look after her, and besides she is very afraid of the Outsider with the Cruel Eyes and the way he laughs at her.

"However, Tula had his own ideas on this matter and he replied, 'I would prefer to wait for Suta, who is yet to mature.'

"I was a little surprised at his apparent determination, but still said, 'Well give the matter some more thought, Tula, and you must hurry and make a decision as the other men are growing restless now, and may not leave Ola alone for much longer.'

"As we can all see now," says Ula, "Tula made the right decision in waiting for Suta to mature and become his partner." Ula nods her head, and the Clan members know the story has finished now. But that dark moon Ula has a restless sleep, dreaming that the Head Scout has returned to live with the Clan.

At sunrise she calls Suta to come and talk to her privately. "I was quite shocked last moon when I could see that the younger Clan members had more interest in hearing about the Head Scout than hearing about Toma," says Ula.

"Yes, I noticed that too," says Suta.

"I do not feel that Toma's memory is properly honoured," says Ula. "I think it could be my fault. I know Tula often mentioned that he thought his fada spent too long watching the Outsider's scouting party, and as a result they spotted him and then ambushed and killed him. I have thought that Toma may have been a careless watcher, and so I have blamed Toma for what happened to the Clan."

"But, Ula, you must remember that Tula also said that he thought the Outsiders were travelling along the river," says Suta. "Even if they had not spotted Toma, they would soon have spotted one of our hunting parties, or someone gathering water at the river. There were many of our tracks at the river, so they would have been watching out for us anyway. Ula, I believe that the Head Scout was such a brutal male that I think he would have always killed whomever he found. He just happened to find Toma.

"I have always felt that Toma actually helped to save the Clan, by deciding to bring back the stone statue of the Mother Goddess. Ula, you then found the statue he was carrying and brought it back to the Clan. In a strange way the Mother Goddess was more helpful to the Clan than to the Outsiders. There is no doubt that your wearing of the statue saved all the Clan children, Tula and the three surviving Clan females. So you see, Ula, Toma really helped the Clan to survive."

Suta watches relief sweep across Ula's face, and her whole body seems to relax. "Meta meta, Suta. For all these full seasons I have felt as though a Great Hairy Beast has been sitting on my back, but after hearing your words, it has gone now. It is such a relief. Of course I can see now that Toma helped saved the Clan. Perhaps you can speak quietly with Fasoma, and after she has had the baba, you can make a special Clan chant to honour this memory of Toma, and tell how *Toma helped the Clan to survive*."

"Of course, Ula. It would make me very happy to do that for you and the Clan members."

"You know, Suta," says Ula, "I think you have always been the most thoughtful and clearest thinker of all the Clan members. Perhaps some moon someone will make a chant about your clear thinking."

"I doubt that, Ula," says Suta smiling very sweetly, "but meta meta for your kind thoughts about me."

11

The Bone Marrow Incident

The next moon Ula is resting when Suta comes over to talk to her. "It has been interesting listening to Faru speak," says Suta. "I have learnt a lot more about the Outsiders now."

"Yes so have I," says Ula. "But I would like to just talk quietly this moon. So if you are not too busy, Suta, go and get Fasoma, and both of you come over and sit beside me."

"I shall do that straight away, Ula."

When both females are sitting down, Ula begins, "I have a matter I would rather keep private from the younger Clan members." The two Clan females know better than to interrupt Ula by asking about the matter, so instead they sit quietly and patiently, waiting for Ula to reveal her private thoughts. As always, Ula starts with other matters first.

"During the cold season I worked very hard to restore a sense of calm and order to life in the cave complex. Three to four times a moon cycle I gathered the Clan members around the large fire to chant our histories, as it was important for the children not to forget these. The Outsiders regularly held their own special ceremonies with their own type of chanting, which Tula told us the Outsiders called 'singing'.

"The Clan children were quite fascinated with this singing and its strange movements. Many times I came across them trying to mimic the Outsiders' singing. But the Clan children's voices are quite different, and I thought they sounded more like the wind howling than singing. However, this activity provided the children with an endless source of laughter. I thought this was a good thing, considering all the pain they had been through recently.

"As well as gathering the firewood and water, the children passed the days learning how to make tools and weapons from the large pile of flint stones and rib bones that were stored in the cave complex. It was important that even the youngest Clan children were taught these skills. The Leader would not allow them to go out hunting, as he said it was far too cold to be away from the cave complex. Certainly the Outsiders only stayed out long enough to make a kill before returning quickly to the warmth of the fire. Faru sometimes sat with Tula and the children making tools too. I noticed his method of making flint hand tools was remarkably similar to the Clan's."

Ula knows that sometimes she starts to wander in her thoughts now. But she really wants to be sure that Fasoma, as a younger Clan member, is given all the history of the Clan's earlier times. She says, "As you well know, life for the Clan has always been ruled by the seasons. In the warmer seasons we gathered herbs, fruit, nuts, berries and mushrooms, and these were either cooked or placed in large storage hides, ready for the colder seasons. When the seasons started to cool, the Clan members were then busy gathering and preparing the woodpile, so that they had enough wood for the fires during the cold season. This was also the time to gather the chestnuts and smoke them, and to sit around the fire roasting them.

"Before it became too cold, we usually sent a party off to bring back the special strong flint stones, which were found far away nearer the mountains. The Clan always had its tasks completed by the time of the hunt of the Great Hairy Beast, which usually appeared just before the cold season. After that, we were busy during the cold season with working on the hides and catching up with our tool making. Well you see, the Clan members had just completed all of our tasks, just when the Outsiders first appeared."

Suta and Fasoma are still sitting quietly, waiting for Ula to talk about the private matter. They notice that sometimes her thoughts seem to jump around from one thing to the next, or go over matters they already know about. However, in Ula's mind she knows there is a certain order in telling a story, and where it is always important not to leave anything out. Ula continues, "Although we had gathered a lot of wood, while the Outsiders were living with us, I noticed the pile seemed to be disappearing faster than usual. Perhaps it was because the two fire hearths were constantly alight. I liked to use the smaller hearth for the Clan children and leave the larger fire hearth free for the Leader and his men.

"I was still very worried about the coldness, having never before experienced such a bitter cold season as this. I was very afraid it might be the start of the great ice covering that is mentioned in some of the Clan's stories from the distant past. I was very concerned, as I just did not know if the Clan would be able to survive living with the Outsiders and living with a great ice covering at the same time." Ula pauses now, and Fasoma and Suta can see that even just thinking about this matter brings a worried look to Ula's face.

Ula lowers her eyes. "It must have been very early in my pregnancy when I first realised I was having a baba. I noticed those vague feelings of extra tiredness and some slight sickness in my stomach. But I did not mention it to anyone, not even to Tula. I remember feeling disappointed it was not the warmer weather, because then I could have collected those little purple berries that females with child are never to eat. Unfortunately, I knew it meant now that I was stuck with the pregnancy unless good fortune intervened. By the time the berries appeared in the warm season, it would be too late to take them."

At first Suta and especially Fasoma are deeply shocked to hear about this, and they can understand why it is best not to talk about this matter in front of the others, especially Fasoma's partner, Tibula. Neither female has ever heard of a Clan member deliberately taking the little purple berries when with child. But Suta speaks up, "We should not be in judgement about such a matter, Ula. You have no need to feel guilty about your thoughts at the time. Besides, you have always been such a good mada to Tibula."

However, Fasoma thinks quietly that Ula always seemed to favour Tula more than Tibula. Although she and Tibula have always accepted this, she never really knew before how much Tibula was not wanted at the beginning. Then she remembers Ula's story about the Leader's approach under the tree. Yes, Suta is right. No one should be in judgement about Ula's thoughts. Still, she decides it would be better never to tell Tibula about this conversation, as he might find it hurtful.

Ula continues, "Unexpectedly, being pregnant with Tibula ended up helping Ola. You see when the Outsider with Cruel Eyes was preparing to leave the cave complex to go and live nearer the river, he asked the Leader if he could take the Clan female Ola with him. Poor Ola was so upset, as you know she was very frightened of him. As well as not wanting to leave the Clan, she did not want to take her little female child away from the other children. She was also worried that once away from me and the Leader, the other men might also want to use her for sexual favours. This sort of behaviour, of course, has always been forbidden in the Clan.

"I asked Tula to explain to the Leader that I needed Ola to help out with the children at the cave complex, as there was too much work for me to do without Ola's help. It was only when I confessed to the Leader that I was carrying a baba that the Leader appeared to listen. He decided it would be better for the Clan female Ola to remain at the cave complex, more to be of assistance to me, rather than just helping with the children. The Leader seemed very pleased to hear that the Mother Goddess was carrying his child. He already seemed convinced it would be a male child, and started boasting about his 'son', as though somehow a male child was more important than a female child.

"After the Outsider with the Cruel Eyes left the cave complex with four other males, Ola was too frightened to ever leave in case she came upon them. Unfortunately that left mainly Tula and me to collect the water now, sometimes with the help of Faru, as neither the Leader nor his scouts wanted to do this task. I was actually quite relieved when the five males left, as this meant there would be less work for me to do now, and also less noise at night. Later in the cold season, we collected ice and snow from outside, which was heated over the fire hearth, and this saved us the work of lugging water up from the nearly iced-over river.

"As you know, Soma was also pregnant, but unlike me was very excited about it, as this was to be her first baba. Already Faru was fussing around her, not allowing her to do the heavy lifting like bringing back the full water hides to the cave complex. It was about seven moons after the sick Outsider had died at the river cave that Soma started having cramping pains."

Fasoma is listening very carefully, as now Ula is talking about her mada. Ula continues, "Soon the bleeding started, and I got Soma to lie quietly on a hide. She was very worried and fretful, afraid of losing the baba. Later during the dark moon time there was a lot more cramping, and finally a little shape was passed from inside her. It was the little unformed baba. Unfortunately, the bleeding did not stop but continued to get heavier. I became very afraid for Soma's life.

"I tried different herbs, but the bleeding still continued until the rising of the sun. Just when Faru and I thought we were losing her, the bleeding clotted. At first there were large clots the size of my hand, until the clotting stopped, and Soma sank into a deep sleep. Later the bleeding became a normal show, but Soma was left in a dreadfully weakened state." Fasoma had known that her mada had lost a baba before birth and had some bleeding, but this is the first time she has heard the whole story. She sits and cries quietly for her mada's pain and loss.

Ula waits until Fasoma stops crying, and smiles gently at her. "I was very worried about Soma but I had an idea to help her. I asked Tula and Ola to meet me at the little fire hearth after the children had gone to sleep. During the meeting I told them how it was only a couple of moons ago that I passed the dead body of the Outsider lying frozen in the snow, and I noticed the body was still intact. It had been taken outside almost immediately after death, and had frozen quickly, so I thought it would still be fairly fresh.

"I wanted to ask the Leader if I could take away the arms and legs from the body. I wanted to cut out the long bones, and make cuts in the bone, so that Soma could suck on them and extract the bone marrow. There should have been enough bone marrow to greatly assist Soma in her recovery. I wanted Tula to tell the Leader that there would not be any further disturbance of the dead body."

Both Fasoma and Suta are now shocked for a second time to hear about this. It is not something a Clan member would normally do to a dead person. "I can see you both look shocked," says Ula, "and so were Tula and Ola at the time. But we were not living in normal times, and I really believed the bone marrow was vital to help Soma make a good recovery after so much blood loss. I was not sure whether the bleeding and clotting might start up again, and if that occurred, we would lose Soma. You see with so few Clan members left, every life was so precious.

"Tula did not like the idea and said that he did not believe the Leader would like the request. Although feeling very uneasy, in the end he agreed when Ola sided with me. It was decided he would be the one to ask the Leader, because of his better language skills.

"That dark moon Tula asked the Leader if the three of us could speak in private, and we moved to the little cave. I was standing beside Tula when he made the request to the Leader. The Leader was so angry he actually raised his hand and slapped me across the head, shouting out, 'Savage, savage,' before leaving the little cave in a rage. I was stunned with this show of anger from the Leader, and was grateful that no others, apart from Tula, had witnessed this outburst against me.

"I can remember saying to Tula in a fit of anger myself, 'How strange to call me a savage. Surely it is the Leader and other Outsiders who are the real savages. After all, they are the ones who left the body of their scout out in the open, fully exposed to the weather and scavenger animals. At least the Clan members respectfully bury our dead to keep the dead bodies out of the reach of scavengers. What heartless people these Outsiders really are. I noticed that night when the sick male died and his body was carried and dumped outside the cave just after death, that there was no Chanting Ceremony or kind words spoken, as is customary with the Clan. In fact there was no sign of grief at all from the other males.'

"Tula had stood there without saying a word, but his brow was deeply creased. I started to realise the seriousness of the situation and quietened down. We were both deeply troubled. We were both thinking that as the Leader had struck me, then could this be thought of as a challenge to my authority as the Mother Goddess? It might mean that life for the Clan could be different now.

" 'Do you think he no longer believes I am the Mother Goddess?' I said to Tula in despair. 'Really, Tula, I do not want to go on anymore pretending to be the Mother Goddess. I am just so exhausted. I think you will have to talk to him and tell him that I am not the Mother Goddess.'

"Again Tula showed his maturity and clear thinking and said to me, 'Let us just wait a few moons and see if things settle down again, Mada. I am not really sure what the Leader is thinking, so let us be very careful not to anger him further as who knows what he may do next.' "

Ula sits quietly with her hands in her lap, waiting for a response from Suta and Fasoma. Neither female has ever heard the story about the bone marrow incident and the hit across the head. They are both wondering what they would have done under the same circumstances. Suta comments, "I never knew you went through these difficult times, Ula. Meta meta for your honesty and courage in telling us about them. It makes you seem even more special now." There is nothing more that needs to be said after these kind words. So the three Clan females sit quietly sobbing and crying, in recognition for the difficult times Ula had to endure, so often in silence.

12

Tula Escapes from the Outsiders

Precious lives were wasted.

It would seem that as soon as the Leader struck the Mother Goddess, he immediately regretted his actions. She had looked deeply into his eyes with a questioning and hurt expression. In fact it was the first time she had ever really looked into his eyes and held his gaze, and he found he was unsettled by the experience.

It was then that he really noticed her eyes for the first time. They were very light coloured and set so deeply into her face that they almost disappeared into her head. Yet still, they were the very thing that pulled your attention to her face. The eyes had a commanding presence, and they looked out over the world in a calm and knowing manner, seeing everything. They were the eyes of a true Mother Goddess. Strange, it was only just then that he thought of how the eyes were missing from the little stone statues of the Mother Goddess. But then no stone statue could ever show her eyes as they really were.

He wished he had not slapped her, but he just could not help himself, as he had felt so outraged and repulsed at the request to allow one of the Clan members to eat his dead guard. This was something unheard of, something that would never happen back at his village. But then, he reasoned, his village was right next to the sea and there was always plenty of fish and other sea creatures to eat. So who knew what someone might do if the circumstances were really desperate enough.

He was so relieved that the whole episode had taken place in the little private chamber, and his men were busy singing, and so would not be aware of what had just happened. He had no intention of ever telling them about it either. He was sure the Mother Goddess was going to punish him after that, and he thought perhaps she would lose his child just like the other Wild Woman had. He considered whether he should say he was sorry for losing his temper, but decided it would be a sign of weakness for a Leader to do so. He would just have to suffer the consequences of his hasty actions, and accept whatever punishment came.

The Leader reflected on the first time he saw the Mother Goddess, when she appeared out of the darkened cave. The first thing he noticed was the look of love and tenderness on her face when she locked eyes on her son. She had never looked at him that way. Indeed her face was always a mask whenever she was with him, and she showed no emotions at all. He wondered what she really thought of him.

The next moon he went down to the river camp to visit his other men, and to invite them up to the cave complex later for a special ceremony. He noticed that the men seemed a little evasive, not making proper eye contact with him. The Head Scout also made excuses for not coming up to the ceremony.

Something about his men's behaviour was very suspicious and it made him think that they must have known about the incident with the Mother Goddess. He did not understand how they could have known about this, as he was the first person to visit their river cave since the incident. Besides, he did not think any of his men witnessed it. He decided that his men's strange behaviour towards him must somehow be the start of his punishment from the Mother Goddess for hitting her across the head. Therefore he decided he would suffer his punishment, and so would not insist they had to participate in his ceremonies. As the moons passed by, he seemed to see less and less of them, and indeed they never came up for a ceremony again.

Faru, knowing nothing of the bone marrow and hitting incident, later told the Clan members how the Leader took him aside and said, "I am concerned about the health of all of my men, including my own health, which has deteriorated during the cold season. Somehow the Wild People have survived in a better condition, maybe because they are used to the restrictive diet and cold conditions. All of my men are having problems with their gums, particularly the ones down at the river camp. I know my men are unhappy living in this harsh climate, although they are too afraid to tell me. I have been doing a lot of thinking, and I have decided I will return home when the weather starts to warm. I want to take back the Mother Goddess to the village and also show off my first child, who will grow up to be a very important person in the village."

Although the Leader had no one to confide in, he was very keen to see if the village Shaman was still alive so he could find out a lot more about the history of the Mother Goddess. There were so many questions tumbling inside his head. He wanted to know how the Shaman first made contact with the Mother Goddess. Faru had told him that when he asked Tula about this matter, Tula had said absolutely nothing. Although Tula had told Faru that all the Clan members, including the Mother Goddess, had been born in the little cave where he slept with the Mother Goddess. Tula also said the Clan members had never travelled more than seven moons' walk from the cave.

So how had the Shaman met the Mother Goddess? How had it all happened? It was baffling, but he could not deny the truth of it all. Still, he needed to know more about the matter and clear his thoughts. Sometimes he was feeling lost and confused, almost as though something was not as it should be. Yes, it was time to return to the village.

* * *

A few moons after Ula has spoken to Suta and Fasoma about the bone marrow and hitting incidents, and given them all time to rest, she decides she wants to continue with the story. So Ula tells them to sit beside her near the fire. "I will start my story this moon where the Leader tells his men and the Clan members that he and his men will be leaving in less than a full moon cycle to return to his village."

Ula continues, "His men looked greatly relieved with the news. Tula told me that the Leader said he wanted me to return with him to his village, but I shook my head violently, and absolutely refused. I said, 'It would be impossible to travel such a long journey while with child, and besides I could never leave the Clan's children as I am their sworn protector.' The Leader accepted my reasons, without any protest. I think he was expecting me to refuse to leave, and besides, he did not want to put at risk the safety of his 'son'. However, when I asked about Tula, the Leader said, 'I have not decided about that yet.'

"Faru immediately sought permission to stay with the Clan, as he was content to live his life with us, especially being so attached to Soma. I was not sure what the Leader would say, but he agreed Faru could stay. However, the Leader made it clear to Faru that if he stayed, then it would be Faru's first duty to look after the Mother Goddess and the Leader's child when born. Faru was made to swear a blood oath that this would always be his first duty.

"The next moon the Leader headed down to the river cave with a couple of his men to give the men there the good news. He was shocked to find the cave empty when he arrived. The fire embers were cold and all their hides and tools were gone. The men had deserted him. He was totally outraged with their treachery, and he swore vengeance. He told us all, 'This will mean death for them should they ever return to my village.' It also meant he would have to take care on his homeward travels, because if he came across them, it would be a fight to the death.

"During the cold season the Leader could see that Tula had grown into a man, and was by far the fittest of all the males. He said to Tula, 'Yes, you will have to come with me now, if we have to do any fighting with the Head Scout, then you will be worth three of my men.' Of course the Leader knew I would not be happy with this decision, but said abruptly to me, 'This is the way it will have to be. Besides, I hope to return again in a few full seasons' time with more men and some females next time too. Tula can come back to the Clan then.'

"The Leader and his remaining men were busy for the next half a moon cycle, sorting the hides, weapons and utensils that they would need to pack for the long journey home. They prepared bundles for the log boat, as well as large packs the men would have to carry. On the last few moons they killed a couple of animals with the soft eyes, which we butchered and wrapped in special wet hides. The packs were heavy and they would all have to be carried down to the old camp site where the men had left the log boat, on the moon they were leaving. The Leader's men were so happy to be going home that they had even taken up singing during the light moon, something the Clan members had not heard them do before. We were greatly relieved the Outsiders would soon be leaving. But Tula and I were particularly anxious."

Ula is ready now to say one of her favourite chants, and she asks Fasoma to see if any of other Clan members wish to join in. She waits till they settle beside the fire, and this time Ula makes an effort to stand as she says the chant. She speaks out in a very strong voice.

The Chant Telling of Tula's Escape from the Outsiders
The day has finally arrived
For the Leader to leave the cave complex.
I embrace my tearful mada,
And all the Clan children are howling.
But unbeknown to others,
My mada and I have made a secret plan.
Just before I leave,

The Leader promises he will return,
As he wants to see his son.
As he walks away he looks back,
But the Mother Goddess just stands there
With the mask across her face.

We are all laden with heavy packs
And it is the Leader's intention
To ferry these in the boat with one of the scouts,
Each day along the river.
However, when we arrive at their old camp site
The boat is gone.
The traitor has taken it,
And the Leader is furious.
Then, calmly with a twisted smile he realises
What fools they are,
The boat will never hold four men and supplies,
It will tip over and they will all drown.

We make camp at the flat rock,
Just where I had hoped we would.
And in the dark moon
When all are asleep,
I gather a pile of belongings
And quietly head for the river.
At the riverside, I open a small container
Of specially prepared fat paste
And smear it across my whole body
From the neck down,
I then fasten my leggings and hides
And wade into the freezing water.

I hold above my head, some food and water
And a set of spare dry hides.
I have to be very careful
Not to slip over,
Because if I wet my dry hides,
I will not survive later in wet garments.
The water is still so cold

That my legs are already numb,
The current is swifter too
Than the last time I made this crossing.
I slip and almost fall
But my precious hides are still dry.

On reaching the other side
I retreat behind some bushes,
And remove the wet hides.
I rub my body briskly
And put on the dry hides,
Then make my way up to the ridge tops
To my old vantage point.
I am still freezing, but cannot light a fire,
And my body still feels numb
When I crouch down
Behind some boulders,
My home for the next few moons.

For two more moons I watch the camp,
As scouts go up and down the riverside,
Looking for me.
They do not cross over the river,
As the Leader knows I hate the water,
Nor does it appear that they have
Returned to the cave complex.
On the third moon, there is no camp fire,
But I still do not light a fire,
Lest they are setting a trap for me.
I wait one more moon
Before deciding to cross the river again.

This time there is no fat paste
To help protect my body from the cold.
And my whole body is so cold
I am numb all over.
I am about halfway across
When I notice a small fire
On the other side.

I feel panic; it is probably the Leader,
What shall I do?
Should I turn and go back?
Someone is now running
Down to the water's edge.

My body is so cold and in pain,
That my mind feels numb too.
I look again,
And I realise the person near the water's edge
Is not the Leader,
It is a female with a slightly swollen belly
Who is holding out her arms to me.
I start sobbing uncontrollably now, choking with tears,
I know it is my mada come to meet me.
Looking at her now,
It is the first time
I think she looks like a real Mother Goddess.

Fasoma can now see that this is Ula's favourite chant. And why wouldn't it be? It is all about the hated Outsiders leaving the Clan members, but more importantly it is about a mada's joy to have her special son safely returned to her.

After the chant, Ula wants to explain more to the Clan members, who have been listening. "I had arrived at the Leader's recently vacated camp site, but I did not relight the fire, in case the Leader was in hiding nearby. Instead I stayed behind cover for two moons, eyes always searching the other side of the river, hoping Tula was over there. As soon as I saw Tula move into the water I started a fire to prepare for his comfort. I watched while he hesitated in the middle of the river and looked as though he may turn back. I rushed down to the water, shouting out to him, desperate to encourage him to continue the crossing.

"When Tula reached the riverbank, I half dragged him back to the small fire and helped him remove his wet hides. He lay on the grass, shivering and exhausted, and I placed dry hides on top of him. I patted down his body strongly, to bring back life to his frozen limbs. I chanted to him and encouraged him to feel better. After some time when his breathing became more regular, I offered him some meat I had brought down from the cave complex two moons before.

"Tula was still resting when I could see he caught a scent in the air, and he looked up just as someone was approaching in the distant shadows. We both gasped, as we thought it might be the Leader come out of hiding. But no, it was Faru who had come down from the cave complex to give help if needed. Tula and I almost cried with relief, and Faru assured us he did not think the Leader would come back now. Faru had brought extra meat and another warm hide, and he wrapped this around Tula and then we all made our way back to the cave complex.

"When we arrived back there was much rejoicing and the Clan arranged a small feast and Chanting Ceremony in recognition of the importance of the occasion. We understood we must capture and remember as much as possible of the recent events, all about the Clan's first contact with the Outsiders. This was surely the most important thing to have occurred in our history.

"During the Chanting Ceremony, Tula informed them all in great detail about what had happened, and how the Head Scout had taken the special boat that the Leader wanted to use to carry his supplies. Faru agreed with the Leader's sentiments that the Head Scout's party would probably get into trouble on the river. He said, 'I can remember a section of the river some distance away where there were some small rapids and the current was very strong. I believe that the Head Scout will be so impatient to return home that he will risk the rapids with the four men and supplies in the boat. I think it will be a disaster, as the boat will most certainly capsize and all their supplies will be lost. The Head Scout is a very strong swimmer so he should survive, and he may even manage to save one or two others.'

"After Faru said that, Ola, looking alarmed, immediately asked Faru, 'Do you believe that if that occurs, it will be likely that the Head Scout or any surviving men will return to the cave complex?'

"Faru earnestly assured her, 'I don't think they will ever return to the cave complex as they know the penalty for their desertion is death, and besides they do not know that the Leader and his other men have also left.' This provided a great sense of relief to the Clan members, especially Ola, who had always been so afraid of the Head Scout, or Outsider with Cruel Eyes as she always called him.

"The conversation then turned to the Leader and what had happened to his party. Tula explained that after he had crossed the river during the night, the Leader and his men spent two moons going up and down the river looking for him. He told the Clan members how he secretly had told me that he would leave the group at the first opportunity. He never had any intention of returning with the Leader to his homeland. It was his secret

101

hope that the Leader would make camp at the flat rock area, just where he did, as it was the best place for him to cross the river. Just as he thought, the Leader had never suspected he had crossed the water.

"Suta asked the Clan members if the Leader was likely to come back to the cave complex, and Faru said, 'I believe the Leader is committed to returning to his homeland, and I doubt if his men would ever agree to come back now anyway. If the Leader does return in the future, it will be quite some full seasons away.'

"Tula then stated with authority, 'I do not believe we will ever see the Leader again.' He later told me how he noticed a faint smile on my face when he said this."

Ula continues, "So it was just after Tula had spoken that I quietly stood up and moved away to the opening at the far end of the cave. Without a single word, I removed my Mother Goddess statue from around my neck, and threw it away into the darkness. At that moment I saw it as nothing more than a piece of rubbish, and I was so relieved to know I would never have to see it again. I closed my eyes, and with reverence remembered my beloved partner, Toma, wise old Myla and all the other Clan members who were killed by the Outsiders. I couldn't help but think of what a waste of precious lives!

"*Precious lives were wasted,*" says Ula.

"*Precious lives were wasted,*" say all the Clan members.

"The next morning the Clan held a special meeting, and on this occasion even the children were invited," Ula says. "We were all aware that once again our very survival as a Clan was at stake, as there were so few Clan adults left alive. The Clan had only me, who was with child, Tula only just reaching manhood, Soma who had only one good arm, Ola, and Faru of course. The next Clan member to reach adulthood would be Suta, but that would still be a couple more full seasons away. That really only left three fit adults available for hunting. But we agreed this should be enough to keep up our food supplies.

"However, as we generally needed eight or nine hunters to successfully kill the Great Hairy Beast, it meant it would be many more full seasons, waiting for all the children to grow up, before we could manage that feat again. Even though we had managed to survive the last cold season without a kill of the Great Hairy Beast, all of our fat supplies were now gone. So we needed to consider how to overcome this problem for the next cold season.

"That point being noted, we then proceeded to the next matter of whether or not we had enough hides still left from the Great Hairy Beast.

Although the Leader and his men had taken some of our hides, we decided we had enough left for our smaller group. We still had some gazzats and knee protectors left over from those Clan members who were killed.

"Probably because I was with child, I said to the others, 'I think the carrying of the water each moon from the river takes up too much time, as we only have three adult hunters who need to be involved with hunting now. I think the Clan should consider moving down to one of the smaller caves near the river, to free up the time spent on carrying the water.'

"Faru suggested, 'What about the cave that the Head Scout lived in?' The Clan nodded agreement and decided that we should all walk down there later and see if the cave was suitable.

"I added, 'It may be possible to keep some of our belongings in the cave complex, or else we could perhaps use a second cave near the river for storage if needed.'

"I was so happy to see that the season was continuing to warm, so that meant the Clan members would be able to pursue our usual seasonal activities. I had been feeling particularly relieved to see the end of the heavy ice and snow. I was always fearful the cold season may just continue on, as told in some of our past chanting history. I still reminded the Clan we would have to make special plans for the next cold season, and be ready early with extra supplies.

"Soma then reminded the Clan, 'Our wood supplies are very low, and at least two Clan members need to take their hand axes and chop wood.'

"I suggested, 'Let's do this after we have decided which cave we will be living in, so that we are not carrying the wood supplies twice. Maybe Soma and I should take out the children to gather the birch bark needed to make the glue for our hand spears and also gather up more herbs. We should also realise we won't be able to make any sopa as usual as we have no fat supplies now.'

"The Clan sat quietly for a few moments and I was deep in thought about not being able to make the sopa, when I had an idea. 'Instead of the sopa, I can later try and make some type of oily paste or liquid using the special herb we use to kill the skin mites, and see if this can be spread over our bodies before bathing.' This idea seemed to make everyone happy, and I think the Clan members appreciated my thinking.

"Ola then asked, 'Can the Clan can spare two hunters to travel to the distant mountains to bring back the special hard flint stones we need?' The Clan decided that the hard flint was still very important, and so this journey had to be made.

"Suta then said, 'I believe I am old enough to make the trip now, and as Ula is with child, and Soma cannot carry a big load with one arm, that leaves only Ola or Tula to go with me.'

"Tula said enthusiastically, 'Although I went with my fada the last warm season for the first time, I remember the way well.' He also stressed, 'Apart from collecting the hard flint there is another reason why I believe it is important to make the trip. The long distance we travel will provide us with an opportunity to try and make contact with another Clan who may be travelling there to also gather these special flint stones.'

"This started an animated conversation about what the Clan should do if Suta and Tula met up with another Clan. Faru suggested, 'We could ask any such other Clan if we could join them and live with them.' And there was some agreement with this suggestion.

"Tula then suggested another idea, 'We could ask the other Clan if our Clan could share in their killing of the Great Hairy Beast so that we might receive a portion of the fat, bone marrow and other parts of the animal.'

"I wanted to calm them down a little and said, 'I think if we meet another Clan then both suggestions could be put to that Clan, and it would be up to the other Clan to decide. But we really need to remember this is only a small possibility, as none of us has ever met another Clan there before.'

"Tula, who was still thinking about the matter of meeting another Clan, said he had another good idea. 'Suta and I should stay away several more moons than usual, and keep a fire going in order to gather the attention of another Clan, if one happens to be nearby. Any sacrifice in time would be worth it in order to meet another Clan and secure a share in the kill of the Great Hairy Beast.'

"On that positive note, the Clan members decided to walk down to the river and inspect the caves. Soma was left at the cave complex to look after the youngest children, and all of the others gathered up a water pouch and off we went.

"Faru led us straight down to the Head Scout's cave, which was probably the largest cave down there. The Clan carefully inspected the cave and believed it would be big enough. I noticed and said, 'We will need to move the fire hearth closer to the entrance so that it does not smoke out the cave. Although there is enough room inside the cave to sleep everyone in rainy weather, we will still clear away some of the brush outside and set up our warm-season sleeping hides.' Nearby we found another cave, which we decided could be used for storage, and further up there was yet another smaller cave that could be used as the birthing cave.

"In less than seven moons, the Clan had moved all that we needed down to the river caves. We had even built a generous fire hearth and set up a large workbench inside the cave, and placed our spare weapons and flint stones, storage containers, spare hides and gazzats in the storage cave. Faru, Ola and Tula took turns chopping wood and doing the hunting each moon. Soma spent most of the time looking after the children, giving them their lessons, and attending to the fires.

"It was probably a strange thing to think about, but I kept thinking just how fortunate it was for the Clan that there were no wild animals to prey on us in the area. We would never have survived if there still had been predators in the area. It was only because over the many Clan generations, the earlier Clan members had ruthlessly hunted and killed the predators, such as the animal with sharp teeth. This was said to be a cunning and dangerous animal, which always hunted in a pack. The Clan's chanting histories tell us that whenever a Clan heard the howling of these animals at dark moon time, then a large hunting party went straight out to hunt and kill.

"I remember talking to Faru about these predators and telling him how the animals had long been cleared out of the area for some considerable distance. In fact no current Clan member had ever heard their howls at night. However, Faru told me that he remembered hearing the howls of the animals earlier during his travels, although he never saw any of them. He wondered if the Leader and the Head Scout might be more vulnerable on their journey home, especially now with their smaller numbers, poorer health and perhaps fewer supplies and weapons." Ula now looks at all the Clan members before saying, "In truth, I don't really like to admit this to anyone, but I was secretly hoping there still might be a few predators out there.

Ula then turns and speaks to Fasoma, "While the Outsiders lived with us, Suta spent a lot of time with me gathering the herbs, the birch bark, and really just trying to learn as much as possible from me." She looks fondly at Suta and says, "Although I had never spoken about it, I did have concerns about the future, and was not sure how things would go with the birthing. I could see that Suta was trying to be ready to take over my duties should anything go wrong. That is why she was spending so much time letting me teach her many things. Suta was outstanding really for someone of only eight full seasons. She already had as much clear thinking as any adult Clan member."

13

The Special Flint Stone

What is best for the Clan always comes first.

Ula is sitting quietly with her legs slightly raised as they seem to be swelling up now. Her thoughts keep drifting back to the past, always back to her story. In her thoughts she can remember that the season was warming, and the green leaves were unfolding in the trees. Down at the river, this green canopy hid the snow-capped mountain ranges, which could always be seen from the cave complex on top of the ridge. So there was no more looking at the fingers of ice moving down the mountain sides. The water in the river was not as cold and icy, and the current not as strong as the time Tula crossed the river.

She is still sitting quietly when Fasoma walks over with Suta, and says, "Ula, is it all right if Suta gives our talk this moon about the special flint stone?"

"That is a good idea," says Ula, "and why not ask some of the younger Clan members as well." Suta rushes off to gather up the younger Clan members, and as usual Ula starts talking to Fasoma, while waiting.

"I remember that Soma asked me if she could speak to me quietly," Ula says to Fasoma. "Soma was looking quite serious and said to me, 'I believe that Ola should also take Faru as a partner. Ola is healthy and it would be best for the Clan if she could also have a child.'

"I said to Soma, 'I understand, but have you spoken of this to Faru or Ola?' Soma said she had not. So I decided to immediately call a meeting for all the adults including Tula as well as even Suta now.

"It was customary in the Clan for an unattached adult to share a partner, but it was really Ola's decision to do so. Ola was aware how devoted Soma and Faru were, so she had not made this request. However, we were all aware that the Clan desperately needed to increase its numbers to be able to survive in the future. So we all agreed it would be best for the Clan for this partnership to take place.

"Faru was hesitant about the idea, so I suggested, 'Perhaps Soma can leave with Tula and Suta on the trek, and this would leave Faru and Ola with some time and privacy to get to know each other better. Anyway, Soma will be able to be useful and attend to the fire and look out for other clans while Tula and Suta find and gather up the special flint stones.' It was agreed that Ola and Faru could make use of one of the little caves while the others were away, and when Soma returned they could work out their own sleeping arrangements between them."

Suta appears now with all the eager younger Clan members, who sit down with her in front of Ula and Fasoma. Suta is looking very pleased to be finally telling some of the story and she begins straight away. "Tula and I were busy making the final preparations for our long trek to gather the special flint stone at the mountain ranges. I remember the moon before Tula, Soma and I were due to leave that Tula stepped forward in a very excited yet rather shy manner. He wanted to show the Clan members an idea he had been working on.

"Tula slowly unrolled a beautifully prepared hide of a baby animal with soft eyes, and then he dipped a thin stick into a container of red ochre paste and started some markings on the hide. He marked the river, the ridges where the old cave complex was located, the Clan's new cave, and at the other end of the hide, the mountain range we would be travelling to. He described how he intended to mark the route on the hide each moon, and add a notch that would indicate each moon's time of travel.

"Faru was also very excited with the idea, and said how much the Leader would have liked it. Tula reminded him, 'It really was the Leader who first came up with the idea when he made those markings in the dirt, the first time he questioned me. I believe it could be useful for the younger Clan members to have this markings hide or *mapa*, as I shall call it. As well as having the Clan's chanting history, it would be helpful to have such a mapa in case something ever happened to the older Clan members.

"'Likewise later we could make another hide mapa to show Clan members where to find the Great Hairy Beast, and any other crucial places of interest that the younger Clan members may need to know.' Tula reminded the Clan members how at risk the Clan children would have been had the other older surviving Clan members also been killed by the Outsiders, for none of the children had yet visited these places or knew the way, as they were too young to travel so far."

The younger Clan members smile broadly as they always love hearing about Tula's clever ideas. Suta continues, "Soma was actually looking forward to the journey. Remember that she had spent so much time recovering from the arm injury and bleeding episode, and after this she had spent all her time at the cave mainly looking after the children. She was greatly missing the daily hunt and company of the older Clan members. She did not feel jealous about the idea of Ola spending time with Faru, or the thought they may have their own baba. *What is best for the Clan always comes first*," says Suta.

"*What is best for the Clan always comes first*," the other Clan members say.

Suta says, "For the first few moons of our journey to gather the special flint, Tula, Soma and I travelled as quickly as possible, and made good ground, stopping only just before moon time. When the food supply was low, we set out at first light to hunt, and after that we headed straight towards the mountains. Each moon Tula marked our progress on the mapa made of the hide of the baby animal with soft eyes, with his coloured ochres. He left it to dry while we slept, before carefully folding it again at first light.

"Once we had moved out of our familiar territory, Tula slowed the pace, stopping to point out places of interest and new landmarks, especially to me, as it was my first journey. Also he wanted to give us the chance to spend some time exploring the new landscape. Whenever we reached high territory we would stop and light a fire, in the hope another Clan might see it, if one happened to be within view. We would wait, and watch the horizon before moving on again.

"A couple of moons later we came across a large cave near the river. It had lots of flints lying on the ground, and a couple of graves. But it was obvious to us that the fire hearths had not been lit for a very long time, and that the Clan had long left the area or died out. Lying outside the cave was a large rock slab made of very hard rock, with strange markings on it. Small holes had been dented into the hard surface, all over it. 'What are those markings?' I asked Tula.

" 'I don't know,' he replied. 'My fada showed me this stone when we were here last full season. He said the stone must have been carried down from the mountain where we are going for the flint, but he had no idea what the markings could mean.'

"Soma said, 'I wonder if a Clan made those markings, or whether it could be the work of the Ancient People, because there is certainly no Clan history of such markings.'

"Soma was quite taken with the cave, and commented, 'You know it was Ula who first suggested the Clan move, the moon after Toma's body was brought back to the cave complex. If we had moved to this cave, then perhaps the Leader would never have found us.'

"Tula replied straight away, 'I think that the Leader still would have found us in this new cave, as he was always following the river. It was really just unfortunate that he had found us back in our cave complex, as he had already decided that in another moon he would move up the river, away from where we were.'

"While Soma was exploring the cave, I had been looking intently at the stone slab, placing my fingertips in and out of the holes. I said, 'It must have taken at least three of the Clan members to lift this heavy stone and bring it here. Also making each hole in such a hard rock required a lot of effort. So I think there must have been a very important reason to have gone to so much trouble.'

"Tula noticed me leaning even closer, and later told me how my nose crinkled as a faint smile lit up my face. I said, 'You know I have an idea what these holes mean. I think it is the history of the Clan who lived here. If you go across the surface then I think each hole represents a Clan member, and if you go down the stone, you get an idea how many full seasons that Clan member lived for.'

"Tula looked intently at the stone and I saw his eyebrows arch with surprise. 'That is a clever idea, Suta, and it certainly is a good explanation. I think I will mark this cave and this special stone on my mapa.'

"When we finally arrived at the base of the mountains where the special flint rock was lying about, Tula and I busied ourselves collecting the flint stones. First I lit a fire for Soma to take care of, and she was left to spend time exploring the area looking for fire hearths recently lit. She was excited when she found one; however, when she showed it to Tula, he said, 'Sorry, Soma, it is the hearth that my fada and I prepared the last full season when we made the journey together.' Soma's smile faded and Tula and I could see she was not able to hide the disappointment she felt.

"After a few more moons, and heavily laden with new strong flint stones, we left for the return journey, very disappointed that there was no evidence of another Clan using or living in that area. We had seen no other dark moon fires whenever our eyes carefully searched the distance.

"When we returned the Clan members gathered around the fire hearth to hear all the news. They were all very interested in hearing about the large stone with strange hole markings. They all agreed with my idea about what it represented, but it was still difficult to try and reason why it was done. Ola said, 'The stone must have been very important to the Clan to go to so much trouble carrying it down from the special flint mountain to the cave and then spending so much time making the markings.'

"'Yes,' I said, 'I think something sad must have happened to that Clan. Perhaps they knew they were all going to die and no one would be left, so they left the stone as a marker that they once lived in that cave.'

"Ola then asked, 'But why would they do that?'

"Ula answered, 'I think when they knew their chanting history was finished they wanted to leave a sign to others who might one day come, that here in this cave lived a Clan, where every Clan member was much valued.' It was a troubling thought as the Clan members realised how easily their Clan might have been destroyed by the Outsiders. They were all wondering what they would have left to tell others of their proud history.

"So it was disappointing for the Clan members to know there were no other clans nearby. It meant the cold season would be harsher for us now without sharing the kill of the Great Hairy Beast. Tula suggested, 'When the Great Hairy Beasts are due to appear in the valley, I could go out as a scout and watch for another Clan who may also be out hunting.' The Clan members agreed this was also probably worth trying, although they considered it unlikely to be successful, as none of us had actually ever seen another Clan, even at that hunt.

"Then Tula proudly showed them his hide mapa, with all his notches and special markings, and everyone was very impressed with it. I remember saying, 'Perhaps Tula's mapa is like the other Clan's stone with markings. It is a part of our history that might outlive us too.' Everyone then seemed happier after I said that." Suta has finished her story now, and stands up ready to move away with the younger Clan members.

Ula has been listening carefully to Suta's story, and says to her, "Suta, before you move away, tell me, how did you decide that the markings on the stone showed the number of Clan members who had lived in that cave?"

This is a very good question, so everyone is listening carefully to hear Suta's answer. "I counted the number of hole markings and there was one full hands and six markings. As our Clan had two full hands and seven Clan members, who were living in a much larger cave before the Outsiders arrived, it seemed to me that this was what the markings were made to show."

"You had very clear thinking for someone so young," says Ula.

Suta blushes a little. "I was very pleased when Tula agreed with me."

Ula leans across and says to Fasoma, "While the three flint gatherers were away, back in the Clan's new cave, Faru and Ola were getting along very well. They went out hunting together early each light moon, and were bonding well. I watched Ola trying to learn how to throw the spear, but just like the other Clan members, she could not manage to throw it nearly as well as Faru."

Ula leans even closer and whispers to Fasoma, "I noticed that on the third moon, Faru entered the little cave where Ola was sleeping. I was quite surprised to hear Ola moaning and later laughing, obviously enjoying his attentions so much. Faru visited every dark moon after that, even sleeping in the little cave until the rising of the sun. How different it had been for me with the time I spent with the Leader. But I was happy for Ola and genuinely hoped that she would find herself with child soon."

14

What Is a Mother Goddess?

The Clan is all about love.
The Clan does not need a Mother Goddess.

Fasoma walks over to Ula and sits down beside her on some hides. Both Clan females have swollen legs and look tired. "Last dark moon I kept thinking about predators," says Ula. "But also I remember Faru once saying how lucky we are not to have any predators any longer. I really like the word 'lucky.' It is one of the new words the Outsiders brought with them, which we now use. Before the Outsiders came, we never had the words, 'murder,' 'rape' or 'prisoner,' as such things never happened in the Clan. These are not nice words, Fasoma, but unfortunately they are part of the Clan's history now.

"But 'lucky' is a very good and useful word. I can truly say that the Clan has been 'lucky' not to have any predators hunting us. Yes the Clan has been 'lucky' that Toma found the Mother Goddess statue, and that I chose to wear it the moon of the great fight with the Outsiders."

"Yes indeed, Ula," says Fasoma, "and 'lucky' for me that my fada took an interest in my mada and lived with us, otherwise I would not be here."

"But the word I like the most is 'love', and I cannot imagine how the Clan existed for so long without having this word," says Ula. "Clan members 'love' each other and the animal families so much. Why 'love' is practically embedded in the Clan's bones. *The Clan is all about love.*"

"Most certainly," says Fasoma. "*The Clan is all about love.*"

"We should get back to the story now, Fasoma, as I can see we both look tired. After Tula, Suta and Ola returned from the gathering of the special flint," says Ula, "the Clan settled back into its normal and busy routine. Both Ola and Soma decided to have their own separate hide tents, and Faru seemed to have a busy time frequently changing his sleeping arrangements between the two. It was clear to everyone that Tula and Suta also got along very well and would, in a couple of full seasons, make a loving couple. I was also enjoying being with child, and really looking forward to having the baba."

"There was a lot of 'love' in the Clan at that time," says Fasoma.

Ula can't help chuckling out loud. "Indeed *the Clan is all about love.* I also remember saying, 'It is strange how the time spent with the Leader already seems so long ago, just like being the Mother Goddess, something only in the past now.' As the weather continued to warm, one day Ola excitedly whispered to me that she thought she might be with child. I just smiled and said, 'I am not surprised with all the noise that goes on in the hide tent at dark moons.'

"It was only half a moon cycle later when Soma spoke to me, saying that she thought she was also with child. This time I immediately suggested that because of her past history, she should take on light duties only. Although I was feeling very strong in my pregnancy, I realised that I was no longer a young female, and so the time had come to take on some of the less strenuous work now, and perhaps have Suta take over my hunting duties."

"I know you never talk about the Mother Goddess, Ula, but would it be all right for Fada to say some words this moon? Some of the younger Clan members have asked about the Mother Goddess."

"Of course, Fasoma. I think that talking of the past is good for your fada, and his memories do seem to be very clear on those matters."

So later after the main meal, Fasoma gathers all the Clan members around the fire to listen to Faru speak.

Faru says, "Meta, Ula, for letting me talk about things that upset you. I know the younger Clan members know little about the Mother Goddess, so I hope my story will be helpful." Ula smiles at Faru, and nods her head, and Faru begins. "One moon Tula and I were out hunting together, and were preparing the animal to take back to the cave, when Tula asked me, 'Will you answer a question that has long confused me? I want to know why the Head Scout cut my fada's throat as he lay dying on the ground.' I dreaded this question, but knew I had to answer Tula.

"I quietly explained how it was a custom in my village tribe, for traitors and cowards to have their throats slashed as a punishment. I said to Tula, 'Because your fada did not try to defend himself, the scouting party assumed he was a coward and thus deserved a coward's death. Of course we now all understand he was never a coward.' Tula nodded his head and accepted the explanation.

"It was then that I asked Tula, 'Will you now answer a question that has long been on my mind? I want to know where Ula's Mother Goddess statue came from.'

"Tula sat very still, pressing his lips together, then looking up at me directly, he said, 'Because, Faru, you really are a Clan member now, I can tell you.' He explained to me simply, 'My mada found the statue beside the dead body of Fada, when we went out looking for him. The Clan had actually never seen a Mother Goddess statue until that day when we brought it back with Fada's body. We had absolutely no idea what it was or what it meant. The moon when the Clan members attacked the Outsiders' camp, my mada just decided to wear it, mainly in remembrance of my fada.'

"Tula went on to explain that while he was held prisoner in the Leader's camp, he observed the Outsiders having ceremonies using the Mother Goddess statue, and he understood then that it was something very important to them. Later after the great fight between the Clan and the Outsiders, when he was brought up to the cave complex, he told Ula to always keep wearing the Mother Goddess statue and pretend she was the Mother Goddess, so as to please the Leader."

Fasoma is noticing her fada looks a little anxious when he says, "I remember when I heard this explanation I was deeply shocked. It was nothing I could have ever imagined. At the time I felt as though someone had just hit me over the head, leaving me so stunned that I was unable even to speak. I was almost sick in the stomach as the realisation slowly dawned on me that the Leader had made a dreadful mistake in believing Ula was the Mother Goddess. She was really just Ula, a Clan member. I could never imagine what the Leader would have done if he had ever found out his mistake.

"Tula also said to me, 'Once my mada wanted to tell the Leader she was not the Mother Goddess, but I managed to persuade her against this idea.'"

"Yes, Tula was very wise to do that, and 'lucky' for us," interrupts Ula. The Clan members sit silently, waiting for Faru to continue his story.

"In the back of my mind, a tiny seed of an idea was appearing," says Faru. "This idea seemed to open up the possibility that if Ula was never the Mother Goddess, then maybe there was really no such thing at all. At this stage I was just feeling quite lost and empty, as I saw part of my faith starting to melt away from me. It was much like observing a Clan member place a lump of fat in a skull container of boiling water, and watching the fat just melt away and then disappear altogether.

"Tula and I then had a long discussion about the Mother Goddess, and Tula asked me to explain what the Mother Goddess is really meant to be. I was able to answer by saying, 'As I understand it, the Mother Goddess is the mother of all the earth and every living creature. I think that is why she is represented with the stone statue as a female with such a womanly body, as it shows her possessing the great fertility needed for the creation of all life.'

"'But equally,' Tula said, throwing up his arms while shaking his head, 'the sun could be said to be a Mother Goddess, because it brings light, warmth and life to all living creatures. Likewise the water could be another Mother Goddess, as it is also essential for all living creatures in order to live. At least with the sun and the water, Faru, you can actually see them. They are real, and you can appreciate what they do for living things. But a stone statue? Faru, it is just that. Simply something made of stone. It is nothing really.'

"'Tell me, Faru,' said Tula, 'before the Mother Goddess, did your people ever believe in another type of goddess?'

"'I really don't know,' I said, 'as I have grown up only knowing about the Mother Goddess, and there has certainly never been any talk of any other.'

"Tula carried on our conversation by saying, 'I think the whole idea of a Mother Goddess does not really make sense, Faru. What is a Mother Goddess anyway? Where does she come from? Where does her magic come from? Where is she now? If what you say is true, then no one has ever seen her. How can you be sure the Shaman has ever really seen her? Faru, you have not really managed to explain any of these things about the Mother Goddess.'

"Tula then slowly scratched his head as he said quietly, and I do believe by now he was actually feeling sorry for me, 'I think the truth is that the Mother Goddess does not really exist. It is probably just a story, made up by the Shaman. Such a story if believed by your village people, as it seems to be, Faru, is a good way of controlling all of the people in your village, to make them obey the Shaman and the Leader.' I nodded, as I saw some sense in what Tula was saying. But it was very hard for me to face this interpretation of something that was the opposite of everything I had always believed in.

"We ended our talk about the Mother Goddess by both agreeing that we were sure the Leader really believed in the powers of the Mother Goddess, and had made a genuine mistake with confusing Ula for the Mother Goddess. I said to Tula, 'I can understand the confusion the Leader must have felt when he saw your mada appear, in such a remote and faraway place, wearing the Mother Goddess statue around her neck. He would have been unable to understand this image in any other way than to consider she was somehow connected to the Mother Goddess, if not the Mother Goddess herself.'

"We then talked about how the Mother Goddess statue ended up beside Toma's body. 'It could have fallen from the Head Scout's belongings when he leant over your fada to slit his throat,' I said.

"'Or else,' Tula said, believing this was the most likely thing, 'Fada found the statue and knew the Outsiders had dropped it, and was bringing it back to show the Clan when he was killed. He probably dropped it himself as he fell to the ground.'

"I concluded the Head Scout probably knew more than he ever admitted. This fact helped me to better understand the Head Scout's strange behaviour, such as leaving the cave complex to live by the river, and no longer joining in the Mother Goddess ceremonies. What I had thought to be simple treachery from the Head Scout was probably more a case of the Head Scout knowing the Leader was wrong in some matters, and perhaps losing some confidence in his leadership. However, all this information was still so confusing for me. I knew I would need to think about it a great deal more, in order to make sense of it."

Faru and Ula are both watching the faces of the younger Clan members. They can see by the children's squinting expressions that it is still hard for them to understand the Outsiders' belief in the Mother Goddess. Fasoma says, "I can understand now, Ula, why you never talk about the Mother Goddess. It must have been very confusing to deal with this strange belief."

"*The Clan does not need a Mother Goddess,*" says Ula in a strong voice.

And all the Clan members say in strong voices, "*The Clan does not need a Mother Goddess.*"

Ula quietly says to Fasoma, "It has been very interesting hearing about this conversation between your fada and Tula. Do you think your fada still believes in the Mother Goddess after all this time?"

"Well I think only a small part of him does now," says Fasoma. "Though I believe this part is all about fear. The fear being that if the Mother Goddess is real, and Fada does not believe in her, then she might punish him for that. I know he no longer has a statue, nor does he ever ask her for anything."

"Meta, Faru, let me just finish the rest of the story now," says Ula. "We are up to the part where all the three adult females are with child. During the warm season, life for the Clan was progressing well, and the time was passing quickly. It had been a very busy warm season for the Clan, as I had insisted we needed to gather double supplies of most items. I was still concerned the cold season would come early and I wanted the Clan to be ready if it did.

"The Clan had devoted a whole small cave to the woodpile, and we had enough wood for two cold seasons. Likewise with the berries and nuts. I had been out with the children each moon to fill up our little containers before taking them back to the storage cave." Faru now calls out that he has something he would like to add to his story, as he realises he has not quite finished. He is becoming nearly as bad as Tula and Ula, wanting to mention everything.

Faru says, "I want to say more about things I noticed about the Clan members, how the Clan adults, and even the children, had an excellent knowledge of the local plants. They knew which plants were poisonous and which plants could be used for food and health benefits. Indeed I marvelled at the hard work all the Clan members did, and how even the youngest of the Clan children set about their tasks, with never a whinge or complaint. The amount of work they achieved was truly amazing. How different things were back in my old village, where the children just seemed to run around most of the time, having a swim whenever they felt hot.

"Things were also different for me back in my village. Even though I was called a guard, there was not really much for me to do. I helped out with making the tools and weapons, did some training in spear throwing, while my main duty was to watch over the Shaman whenever he held one of his ceremonies. When the Leader wanted some guards for the expedition I jumped at the chance to go and have a real adventure.

"However, living here with the Clan, I have absorbed some of your calmness, and I have felt truly useful and needed for the first time in my life. This was even more the case when the three adult females were all pregnant, and so all having to do lighter duties. I spent most of my moon with Tula, while Suta seemed to spend half her time hunting with us, and the other half helping Ula.

"I was just starting to learn quite a lot about the different plants and herbs from the Clan members, although my language skills were still very poor. Tula had started giving a language lesson to the Clan children each dark moon, helping them to learn more of the Outsiders' language. Now that the Leader was gone, Ula seemed quite happy about this.

"Ula had just finished making her special oily substance to kill the skin mites, and the next moon everyone was going to the river to bathe in the shallows. They rubbed the special oily substance all over their bodies just after sunrise and later washed it off. Ula was very pleased with the results, and thought this new method worked even better than the old sopa did. They then washed half of the hides with the oily substance, and after these had dried in the sunshine, they then washed the rest.

"I had become an expert at making the flint hand weapons, and was making good progress with producing the black glue that binds the hard flint rock to the wooden spear stick. I used some of this material to make some more of my throwing spears, and continued to give lessons to the Clan members, who still did not seem to be able to throw very well. I came to the conclusion that the Clan members' shoulder joints must be made differently from those of my people, because with the throwing of the spear, it was more a matter of doing it the right way, rather than just having strength. There was no question the Clan members had a much greater strength.

"Ula had prepared a small cave as the birthing cave, where the pregnant females would give birth and then rest with the babas for a number of moons afterwards. All of the females were having good pregnancies, and even Soma looked happy and healthy this time. I really thought I was the luckiest man alive having two such wonderful and devoted partners, and I couldn't wait to be a fada with my own children.

"Sometimes I thought about the Leader and the Head Scout, and wondered how their journeys home were going, and whether or not they were still alive. Like Tula, I was more inclined now to think the Leader would never return to the Clan's territory. After all, the last journey was such a disaster, with the death of so many men, that I doubted the Leader could manage to get a large party ever again. It would be especially difficult after those in the village heard about the bitterly cold winters and the 'Wild People'." Faru always smiles to himself when he says these two words.

Faru continues, "From time to time I have thought about the differences between my people and the Clan's. To me the Clan members just seem so kind and good, whereas my people seem to be more a mixture of the good and the bad. Of course I see myself as a good person. I include my qualities of kindness, loyalty, being loving, trustworthy, hard working, all really much like the Clan members themselves. Perhaps that is why I felt so at home with you, even right at the start.

"Then I would consider the people in my village. Firstly the Leader, who was harsh, conceited, ambitious, ruthless, selfish, but still had good qualities such as concern and loyalty to his men and the Mother Goddess. But things started to get worse when I thought about the Head Scout. He was cold and cruel, and had no concern for others at all. He was a traitor too, with no real loyalty to his Leader or the other men. However, when I thought about the Shaman, I had to agree with Tula's thoughts. Yes indeed, the Shaman was a dangerous person, who ruthlessly used the poor village people, all for his own gains and power."

15

The Bison Hunt

Planning is necessary,
Planning is everything,
Contentment is happiness.

Ula has noticed that her body somehow feels different now. Her legs are still swollen and it is hard to move around. Also she notices the liquid does not flow so easily from her bladder anymore. So she prefers to rest on some hides, closing her eyes quite often. The talking with Fasoma seems to leave her feeling exhausted, but she wants to continue just a little longer. Every time she talks to Fasoma, it is as though the talking steals some of the life from her body. Once she has told Fasoma the story, her thoughts on that matter seem to vanish, as though gone forever.

Perhaps this is what dying is all about. You have to give up your body and your thoughts, everything just leaving, in its own time. Ula thinks that when she is finally dead, she will be like one of the animal hides, lifeless, but somehow still here. Or perhaps her love for the Clan and her Clan members will live on forever, somehow embedded in her bones, which will probably lie buried in one of the caves.

Fasoma has noticed that Ula seems much weaker, and she has become very worried about her. When pressed, Ula says she wants to keep telling the story, but will end at Fasoma's own birth. "After that it will be your story to tell, Fasoma," she says. "Perhaps later this moon we should invite the Clan members to listen to the story about the bison hunt. It has always been a favourite story they like to hear. Maybe you can ask Suta to tell this story also, for after all she took part in the hunt.

"Although before the bison hunt story, I should tell you about the birth of my baba, for after all, Fasoma, you will be having your own baba very soon. Well I was about to have the baba any moon. However, I still wanted to call one last meeting before the birth, so that the Clan members could go over our plans for how to survive the next cold season. We needed to make sure we had not missed anything in our planning."

"*Planning is necessary*," says Fasoma.

"Yes, *planning is necessary*," says Ula. "You see, Fasoma, I was convinced it was most likely to be another tough, cold season for the Clan, especially with three new madas and babas. This was going to leave only Tula, Faru and Suta to be the hunters. The Clan definitely needed to have everything very well prepared, so that these three would be free to do the hunting for the Clan each light moon.

"At the meeting we discussed what had been achieved: yes, we had a good wood supply; yes, we had collected a good supply of summer herbs, fruits and nuts; yes, we'd had our special baths and washed all the hides; yes, we had a good supply of flints, some of which had already been made into weapons. Actually we had more than enough special flints for a couple of full seasons, and would not have to send out a flint party the next full season.

"However, we had not solved the fat problem yet. Tula would later be going to the grazing valley of the Great Hairy Beast to see if any other clans were about. He would have to do this task on his own, as the Clan would definitely need at least two hunters back at the caves to hunt for the Clan.

"Indeed, as we thought about what we had achieved, the Clan members were more than a little proud that we had managed to be ahead of where we would have been normally. This was really quite remarkable, considering our diminished numbers. It showed what a good job we had done to ensure our survival. Yes, there was some luck, but mostly our survival depended on a lot of good planning and hard work.

"A few moons later I told everyone that the birthing pains had commenced and that I would go up to the special cave I had prepared for the birth. This is the same cave you will be using, Fasoma," Ula points out. "I asked Suta and Ola to stay up at the little cave with me. When in the cave, I crouched in a half sitting position, supported by the two, and I asked them to rub my back and chant quietly. I did not moan even when the pain was strong, as it all seemed very normal and really did not trouble me. Suta was so thoughtful, and she just seemed to know when to dab cold water across my face or offer me a drink of water.

"I was so surprised when the baba came quite easily, as for some reason I was expecting a difficult birth. After the birth I was even feeling strong enough to cut the chord myself, and after the baba cried, I placed it straight on my breast. It was a moving and beautiful experience for the three females to witness. My only feeling of regret was that Soma was not there as well to share those precious moments, although she was waiting around not far away from the birthing cave.

"I was a little surprised to see it was a male baba. The Leader was right after all; he always insisted it was a son. I looked at the little naked baba, with long legs like his fada and brown skin, not quite as dark as his fada's though. It was then I decided to name him Tibula, to honour the fada he would probably never meet. This was the right thing to do. Yes, I was fortunate, Fasoma, to have such an easy birth, and I hope this will be the case for you too," says Ula, but looking away as she says this.

Ula continues, "After the birth and naming of Tibula, Suta and Ola left the cave to go and give the good news to the others. There was much shouting and whooping for joy, and even though it was well past sleep time for the children, those who had fallen asleep were woken up and given the good news. Soma and Tula brought out a small feast they had already prepared, and so began a Chanting Ceremony to celebrate the happy occasion.

"I only spent a few moons in the cave with Tibula before I felt ready to move back to my hide tent next to the others. The baba was feeding well and sleeping quite soundly, and already everyone in the Clan had fallen in love with him. My easy birth gave a great deal of confidence to Ola and Soma, who were now hopeful things would go well for them too, when their time came to give birth in a couple of moon cycles."

"That was such a lovely story, Ula," says Fasoma. "It gives me great comfort that I will have a good birth too. Why don't you rest now and I will gather up Suta and the other Clan members, and Suta can tell her story about the bison hunt."

"*Contentment is happiness*," says Ula.

"Yes," says Fasoma, "*contentment is happiness. The Clan is everything.*"

As soon as the Clan members finish their main meal, Suta gathers them all around the fire, ready to begin her story. One of the Clan children asks, "Suta, why doesn't the Clan have a special chant about the great bison hunt?"

Suta looks across to Ula, who smiles and throws up her arms in the air. "Perhaps after telling her story this moon, Suta will decide to make a special chant," says Ula. "These Clan children ask far too many difficult questions, but they are fair questions all the same," says Ula. "Well, Suta, will you make a special chant in the future?"

"Why yes, Ula," says Suta, "but you must give me enough time to think about it first, as I am not clever at making chants like Tula used to be. I remember he could make a chant in just a moon."

Suta begins, "When the warm weather was almost finished, the Clan decided to hold a meeting to work out the final preparations for the coming cold season. We had still not solved the problem of how to face the cold season without any fat supplies. Although Tula would go out scouting later when the Great Hairy Beast arrived, the Clan still believed it was a faint hope that he would come across another Clan.

"It seemed that for some time Tula had been wondering if they should hunt the animal with fatty neck, which arrived in the valley a moon cycle earlier than the Great Hairy Beast. While this animal did not have the rich fat layers of the Great Hairy Beast, it did have a thick layer of fat across its neck.

"The Clan members had a lot of discussion about hunting the animal with fatty neck. We finally decided that it would take a minimum of three hunters to bring down one of them, which would mean that all the three remaining hunters, Tula, myself and Faru, would have to leave the Clan for about seven moons. This would leave the Clan with just one potential hunter, Ula. She was really too busy with her new baba, and Ola and Soma were both heavily pregnant and not really fit enough to go hunting each moon now.

"Soma suggested, 'We should send out the hunters now to hunt some extra animal with head bones, and smoke the meat back in the small cave of the old cave complex. The smoked meat would have two useful purposes, the first being that the three hunters of the animal with fatty neck could use it. They could carry some of this meat with them and thus free up their time from hunting for food each moon, to concentrate on just hunting the animal with fatty neck. The second purpose is that the smoked meat would be available for the rest of the Clan back here in the cave, while the hunters are gone.'

"Everyone saw this as a very good idea, and even though we preferred fresh meat to smoked meat, the smoked meat would be suitable for a couple of moon cycles. So it was decided that the hunters would spend extra time hunting the animal with head bones immediately, to prepare and smoke the meat, and be ready to go out in the next new moon cycle to hunt the animal with fatty neck. Faru had never hunted this animal, and seemed quite excited about it. He said he would take along some of his newly prepared, strong throwing spears.

"So it became a very busy time for the Clan members. The three hunters went out early each moon and after seven moons we had killed four animal with head bones and carried them back up to the old cave complex. Here Ola, Faru and I butchered the animals and set up the smoking chamber around the smaller fire hearth. It was decided that Ola would stay up there for the next two full hands of moons, while Faru and I would take turns in staying with her. After the meat was properly cured, the three hunters would make a few trips, carrying it back to the new cave.

"When the time came for the three hunters, Tula, myself and Faru, to leave for the hunt of the animal with fatty neck, I can remember that both Soma and Ola were tearful. Although it was still a full moon cycle before Ola's baba was due, and a little longer for Soma, the Clan members knew one could never be sure with these matters, and so it was hard to have Faru going away at such a crucial time. Also, the hunt of the animal with fatty neck was quite a dangerous activity, as normally five hunters would be sent, so the risk of injury for the three hunters was also very real.

"The three hunters set off with a selection of weapons, a water hide each, some hides to be used as camping tents, some slings to carry home the animal with fatty neck, and enough smoked meat for seven moons. On the second moon, we split up and headed out to try and locate the herd. Tula was the one who smelt and found their droppings, and then followed their tracks. These led to where the animals were grazing in a narrow valley, at the end of which was a rocky escarpment.

"Later Tula told us how he had an idea in the back of his mind. He skilfully made his way around the herd without their awareness of his presence, and carefully examined the escarpment and layout of the land. The valley narrowed near the escarpment, which dropped away about three times the height of the animals. Tula thought that if the herd could be frightened and stampeded towards the escarpment, then for sure some would fall over the edge. Any injured animals would then be easily killed, with little risk of injury for the hunters.

"He quickly made his way back to the meeting place to tell the others. That dark moon we sat around our small camp fire and talked about his idea, and we decided it was a good idea, and worth a try. The whole success of the plan would depend on getting the animals to stampede in the direction of the escarpment. Faru suggested, 'Why don't we use fire to frighten the animals?' Agreeing to this suggestion, we set out at the rising of the sun, and just like Tula did on the previous moon, we carefully examined the area and the escarpment.

"We decided to start the ambush just as the sky started to darken, so that the fire would look threatening to the animals, but there would still be some dim light for all to see. Faru would later position himself on some boulders near the escarpment, and would use his throwing spears when the animals approached, aiming just for one or two of them. The three hunters would set up some brush fire hearths close together to present a barrier of flames. Faru suggested we clear some of the grass behind the fire hearths, so that the fire would not get out of control. Once the fires were lit, Tula and I would run towards the animals shouting and waving fire sticks. The animals should be startled, and hopefully when they saw the fire barrier nearby, they would then run off towards the escarpment.

"The plan was risky for Tula and me, because if the animals ran the wrong way, there would not be much time to escape the stampede. So we carefully checked out places where we might be able to take cover."

"*Planning is everything*," said Ula.

"Yes," Suta agreed. "It has always been. *Planning is everything*. We then started preparing the fire bushes and torches, and silently carried them into position. Faru set off to also get in a good position. Just before the fading light, Tula and I lit the fires, and with much shouting and hooting we ran towards the startled herd.

"The animals took off in all directions, some running straight at Tula and me, and some stopping and turning when they saw the fires ahead. Tula and I both scrambled for cover, either behind or up a tree when a number of the herd passed. Then we set off down the valley, chasing the others towards the escarpment. More confusion ensued with animals changing direction frequently, but about six animals headed straight towards the escarpment.

"Faru was ready with a pile of throwing spears and managed to injure one animal that stopped short of the escarpment but then just seemed to fall over. It was followed by two more animals that rushed straight after the first one, while the other three changed direction and headed away. Faru did not even have to throw a spear at the second and third animals, which broke their legs with the fall, and lay injured and moaning loudly.

"By the time Tula and I arrived at the escarpment, we were laughing deliriously. Never had we had such a successful hunt and not a single injury. It was truly unbelievable! We quickly slipped down the rocks and killed the three injured animals, to end their pain and suffering. Then we made our way back to where we had started the fires. We beat out the flames with a hide, and gathered our tools, which had been stored in a safe place.

"We returned to the three animals with fatty neck and made a fire at the bottom of the escarpment. We worked through the dark moon butchering the animals and preparing the parts of the animals we wanted to take home. We considered it a great pity to leave behind so much of the three animals, but we had no other choice with only three Clan members to carry the load back to the cave. So we decided to take back the hides, bones to supply the marrow to the females with child, the best cuts of the meat and the fat, of course.

"We removed the hides from the animals, and used one hide to prepare the sling in which we stacked the parts of the animal we would take back to the Clan. Tula then said to Faru and me, 'I believe the cave we have slept in will provide a good camp site for when I return soon to watch out for the Great Hairy Beast, and also for the next hunt of the animal with fatty neck, if we have one the next full season. I would like to stay an extra couple of moons and properly prepare a hide and a wood supply for storage at the cave.' Faru and I agreed that this seemed like a good idea, and although the sling would be a heavy load for the two of us, we set off. Tula was left behind to later bring home the spare hides, tools and precious fat supplies.

"There was great celebration when Faru and I arrived back at the cave after the hunt. Everyone was certainly very relieved that there had been no injuries. That night the Clan members had a feast of fresh meat to celebrate such a successful hunt. Faru was very impressed with the hunting of these large animals, which he named 'bison.'" Looking across at Ula, Suta smiles and says, "I remember Ula was very pleased to know she would soon have some fat ready for the cold season."

Suta continues, "At the last moment just before leaving the escarpment cave, Tula decided to leave behind his hand axe and other tools, as well as the two hides. He thought it would be useful to have these stored in the cave. They could be carried home after the next visit if needed. He was anxious to return to the Clan with the fat supplies as quickly as possible, and knew he would travel more quickly with a smaller load to carry."

Suta has finished telling her story about the bison hunt. Everyone is now busily chattering, so it is obvious to Fasoma that the Clan members have greatly enjoyed Suta's story. Fasoma walks across to Suta and touches her arm gently as if to say "meta meta". She notices Ula's eyelids are looking heavy, and she is pleased to notice that Ula also looks content. This moon's stories have managed to provide Ula with some happy thoughts and memories.

Just as Fasoma thinks Ula is about to fall asleep, Ula suddenly startles and sits up, leaning on one shoulder, and calls out, "Fasoma, bring over Suta. There is something I wish to say." The two Clan members sit beside her, propping an extra hide behind her, and Ula says, "Suta, I need to tell you what clear thinking you had for someone so young."

"But you have already said that before, Ula."

"But, Suta, you were so mature for someone of just eight full seasons, and your thinking has always been clear."

Ula looks across to Fasoma now, smiling and shaking her head, then she smiles at Suta. "Suta, you have always been so shy, so different from Tula, who always had so many words to say, while you say few. But, Suta, you have always been so mature and clear-thinking. I am so happy that you and Tula had a wonderful partnership, with so much love."

Ula looks back at Fasoma now and says, "When the Leader and other Outsiders lived with us, Suta would spend half the moon with me trying to learn everything I knew. Suta would ask me, 'What is that used for, Ula? How do you make that, Ula? Will you show me that, Ula?' She was trying so hard to learn everything I knew. She was mature enough to understand that something might happen to me during the birth of my baba Tibula. So she set about to learn enough to be able to take over my duties, should I die. I never asked her to do this. Who would ever expect a child to do this much?"

Ula looks back to Suta now. "But meta meta, Suta. I have loved you as my own female child." After these words all the three Clan females are crying.

Suta says, "Meta meta, Ula, after my mada was killed by the Outsiders, I have loved you as a mada too. You did so much for the Clan, Ula. I was only ever trying to help you. I was lucky to have Tula as a partner. *Contentment is happiness,* Ula."

"Yes," the three Clan females say tearfully. "*Contentment is happiness.*"

16

The Birth of Fasoma

Life Brings Death,
Death Can Give Life.

Fasoma has been resting up in the birthing cave, as the time for the birth of her baba is nearly due. She walks down to the main cave, as it will soon be time for the meat meal. She is surprised to find Ula lying on some hides right next to the fire hearth. "Are you not well, Ula?"

"I was feeling very cold and tired so they moved me closer to the fire. You are also looking very tired, Fasoma. I can see dark shadows under your eyes. I think you should be resting more too."

"Honestly, Ula," says Fasoma. "Tibula tells me if I rested any more that my legs would forget how to walk. Ula, if you are feeling too tired, I can come back next moon for more of your story."

"No, stay, Fasoma," says Ula. "I would like to finish my story now, as it is almost ended anyway. We are up to the part where Tula had returned from the bison cave.

"About one full hands of moons after Tula returned from the bison cave, the weather suddenly became much colder. There was no doubt that the cold season had started even earlier this full season, and the Clan was now expecting it to be even more bitterly cold. Faru reminded everyone, 'It was at this time the previous full season that the Leader and the Outsiders first appeared, and it was not as cold as this then.'

"Now that Tula was back, Faru stopped the daily hunting, as he was too anxious to leave the two pregnant Clan females. Ola's baba was due any time now and it was just a matter of waiting for the pains to start. Sure enough the next moon she started having some pains, and so was moved up to the special birthing cave. I arranged for Suta and Tula to help out Ola at the birth, as I needed some time to feed my own baba. But I still intended to keep an eye on things. Soma was allowed to watch the birthing so she could get a better idea of what to expect when her time came.

"Ola's birthing was quite long, and went all through the dark moon. Everyone felt exhausted when she finally gave birth to a healthy baba girl. The little baba was carefully wrapped and taken down to the cave to show to Faru and the Clan members, and then Faru brought the baba back to Ola for feeding. Faru was so overcome with joy and relief that he was actually crying with happiness. The Clan adults were just feeling too tired to hold a feast, so instead we had a small Chanting Ceremony to honour the happy occasion. In about two full hands of moons, it would be Soma's turn to have her baba.

"A few moons later, Tula called a meeting of the adults as he believed it was time for him to go to the big valley and look for the Great Hairy Beast and any other Clan hunters. I did not want him to go. I said at the meeting, 'We have enough fat for the cold season now, and the moons are too cold anyway to be out alone.'

"Faru also thought Tula should stay, and he said, 'I do not want to do any daily hunting as I am busy looking after Ola and the baba, and want to be around for Soma's birth. Soma seems very nervous about the birth. Besides, if Tula goes it will mean the Clan will really only have Suta to do the daily hunt.'

"Tula stood his ground and said, 'I believe it is important for the Clan to try and meet with other clans whenever they can, and the hunt for the Great Hairy Beast only comes once a full season.' He assured the Clan, 'I have excellent supplies in the bison cave, and only intend to stay away for three or four moons. Besides, the Clan will still have a good supply of smoked animal with head bones and some bison left, and can survive on that.' With some reluctance the Clan agreed he could go. Because I was so worried, I insisted he take his leggings and full winter hides as the weather was so cold now, and there was a strong possibility of early snow.

"Tula set out, and on the second moon he looked down on the valley from a high vantage point, but could see no activity in the valley. Later when walking through the valley, he was shocked to discover the droppings and tracks of the herd. It appeared the herd had not only come early, but had also left very early that season, perhaps as a result of the cold. Also, there was no sign at all of any sort of Clan activity in the valley, so he realised it had been a wasted trip. Disappointed, he headed back to the bison cave to camp before returning to the Clan at first sunrise.

"During the dark moon, the conditions deteriorated badly, and it started snowing and the wind started to howl. When he looked outside the cave he could barely see his hand before him, so he realised he would be stuck in the cave until conditions improved. He was so thankful to have the warm bison hides, tools and good wood supplies, as he realised he may be there for a few moons. He knew I would be upset and worried about him. He felt concerned, realising how much the Clan needed him, especially if Soma started birthing early. If that happened, then Suta would be required to help out with the birthing, and the Clan would be without a hunter. Yes, he thought, he should have listened to his mada's wise words and not come.

"For four moons he stayed in the cave because of the bad conditions. The next sunrise the wind had died down and the snow was falling only lightly. He grabbed only his hand spear and water pouch and, dressed in his winter hides and leggings, headed off. He reached the Clan's cave after dark, and everyone was very relieved to have him home safely again. He apologised to me and the Clan for any anguish he may have caused.

"The Clan was very surprised to hear about the early arrival and departure of the Great Hairy Beast. We believed that this must have been connected to the recent change to an earlier and colder cool season, somehow bringing about a change in the herd's movements. We realised that even if we still had all of the original hunters, this season we would have missed the actual hunt, with these earlier movements of the animals. So Tula's journey had resulted in some useful information for the Clan. We were also left wondering if the same situation may have occurred for other clans living in more distant places.

"Tula and Suta quickly established the routine of setting out hunting at first light, and if needed, Tula then went back alone as the sky started to darken, to hunt for animals coming to the river for a drink of water. Unlike the Outsiders, who were always lazy hunters, the Clan members did not like to hunt in just one area, and so in the past and even now, the hunters travelled off to different locations on a regular basis. The aim had always been to try and kill only a few members of each animal family so that we did not kill off the animal families."

"As it has always been," says Fasoma. "*You never kill an animal family. You never kill a herd.*"

"This has been our lifelong method of hunting," says Ula.

"Yes," says Fasoma, "and by this method the Clan members have learnt to have a good understanding of the number and types of animals living in our whole hunting area. Thus we would never kill an animal unless it was absolutely needed, nor would we ever kill the last breeding male and female pair of the herd. Such has been our Clan's method of hunting, that a great deal of the hunting time is actually spent on locating the animals and checking on their welfare. The news of their location and well-being has always been taken back to the fireside for discussion each dark moon."

"It was really shocking, but the Outsiders, when living in their cave near the large flat rock, killed many of the animals with soft eyes. "They were such lazy hunters," Ula says again, almost moaning, "always going for the quickest and closest kill. They were not interested in the health and welfare of the animal herd. They had even killed the main male animal of the herd, something we would never do. That meant it would be a few full seasons before one of the young male animals would grow to take over this role. So for the Clan that meant no hunting of this particular herd for some full seasons." For a moment Ula's eyes flare with anger at the memory of such a needless slaughter. "*The animals are family. The animals are family,*" she says, looking very distressed. Fasoma quietly pats her arm to calm her.

"I remember at that time," says Ula, "that the Clan adults were extremely concerned about whether the colder weather would affect the animal families. So we decided that the hunters would need to monitor the animal families even more closely. So we were watching to see if their food supply and grazing habits were changing, and if the animals still seemed to be breeding normally."

"Yes, we are still doing that now, Ula," says Fasoma. "For now we think everything looks as it should be, but we are still concerned. Should the seasons become any colder, we think we will be in trouble then. For now the animals are still breeding normally. We still have the warmth in the warmer seasons, so there is still plenty of grazing food for them. Though they are suffering a little in the cooler seasons, we notice."

Ula nods and seems to settle down now. She looks up and smiles at Fasoma. "Your fada named the animals with soft eyes, deer. I remember a story about a baba deer that I must tell you. For some reason it is very special to me. One light moon when Tula was out hunting with me, we came across a baba red deer that had a badly broken leg. It was lying on the ground making little bleating noises and the mada deer was standing nearby, looking distressed. The mada deer was startled and ran away as Tula and I approached the injured animal. But she still stayed close enough to watch us make a strong little splint, which we bound to its leg.

"When we returned a couple of moons later, the little animal was still lying there, but looking much sicker. This time the mada deer moved only a short distance away as we approached. Tula told me how he remembered the saddened animal looked deeply into my eyes. It was as though the mada deer understood what had to be done. Tula watched me silently take my sharpest flint, and cut the throat of the baba deer to quickly bleed it out, and so end its suffering.

"Then Tula picked up the lifeless body and carried it on his shoulders back to the cave complex. He skinned the animal and spent a lot of time preparing the soft little hide with his lizzwa. He said to me, 'One moon I shall make something very special with this hide,' and so he carefully put the hide away until the moon he brought it out to make his first mapa for the Clan."

"That is a lovely story, Ula," says Fasoma. "I can see now why you treasure Tula's mapa so much."

"When I die," says Ula, her voice almost fading away, "then you should give the mapa to Suta."

"Of course, Ula, but you should not talk about such sad things," says Fasoma.

"*Life always brings death*, Fasoma."

"Yes, Ula, it is so. *Life always brings death.*"

"Well it is time to finish the story, Fasoma, as your birth chant will be the end of my story. Come close. Let us talk quietly," says Ula. A hand with cold, ragged, white fingers, looking as though they have reached out from the snow-capped mountains, latches onto Fasoma's shoulder. It pulls her towards Ula. A voice, barely a rasping whisper, starts speaking to Fasoma. There seems to be much urgency now in Ula's voice.

"Back in the cave, Soma was becoming increasingly impatient and worried about the birth of her baba. She confessed to me she had been having bad dreams at night, and these had unsettled her. I promised her all would go well. I reassured her by saying, 'Just look at Ola and me. We have both had a normal birth and beautiful babas. I will tell you now I was very afraid when my time came to give birth, although I did not tell anyone this then.'

"Even though I was so healthy during the pregnancy, I told Soma that I still thought it was possible I might give birth to a dead baba. You see, Fasoma, I was not at all sure what would happen when two different types of people mate. We all know the red animal with soft eyes never mates with the brown animal with soft eyes. So was it going to be the same when someone with red hair and pale skin mated with someone who has brown skin and comes from a faraway place? But see, it has all worked out so well.

"Soma said to me, 'Meta, Ula. That makes me feel a little better, but I still worry that the bleeding might start. I would hate to give birth and then not live to see my baba.'

"Again I reassured Soma, 'I doubt if you will bleed again like last time, as I think that time the baba was not meant to be born. Besides, you have not lost a drop of blood this time. I will make sure I am with you during the birth, Soma, so do not be too worried. When the time comes I will give my baba to Ola to suckle so I can look after you.' Fasoma and Ula are close to crying again now. They both know the next part of the story.

Ula takes a couple of deep breaths through her nose. The meat on the fire hearth is nearly cooked now, but something is terribly wrong. Ula cannot smell the delicious fragrance of the meat, and she knows it is her favourite: the animal with soft eyes. She sighs softly. It is well known amongst Clan members that as the body prepares for death, the sense of smell disappears. Ula is surprised, as this has happened so quickly. She realises now she must be closer to death than she thought.

Her eyes are worried and fretful, and Fasoma is looking at her with great concern. "That's enough for this moon, Ula. You can rest now. I can say my own birthing chant. Rest now, Ula. You have done well remembering all these stories you have told me and the other Clan members. I shall remember and treasure them always."

Ula is feeling even more agitated and confused. She is becoming very tired now, but is trying to remember something very important. Trying so hard to remember something very important, something, something about courage. Meanwhile, Fasoma takes her hand and softly whispers her own birthing chant.

Birthing Chant of Fasoma
Twelve more moons have passed and
The time has come for Soma
To move up to the birthing cave.
Ula has given her baba to Ola to suckle,
As she has promised to stay with Soma.
Suta has lit a fire outside,
And Tula's job is to keep it burning strongly,
As the night is so dark and cold.
The birth is progressing normally
Until Ula notices the first trickle
Of bright red blood
Running down Soma's legs.

She asks Soma to lie down on a thick hide
And examines between her legs.
There should not be blood now
As the baba is not yet emerging.
Something is wrong,
And Ula does not understand what is happening.
Soma and Suta see the worry
In Ula's eyes,
And Soma is starting to whimper.
Tula is now standing erect like a guard outside,
Watchful and attentive
Body tensing as though for the hunt.

Suddenly the blood is running,
No longer just a trickle.
Soma is sobbing softly
And Ula gently rests another hide under her.
Ula has never seen this happen before,
Although she is aware
That sometimes bleeding comes after the birth.
Soma is agitated and wanting to stand up,
But Ula tells her to lie still,
And she gently dabs her face
With cool water.
Soma is starting to feel faint.

The blood is almost gushing now
And everyone knows how it will end,
As the bleeding is not going to stop this time.
Soma looks into Ula's eyes,
And with urgency says,
"Ula, you must save the baba.
It would be wasteful
To lose both mada and baba.
Ula, you must promise to act
And do whatever you must do
To save the baba."
The bile is moving up Ula's throat.

There is so much blood,
So much blood,
And Ula takes Soma's hand
And says, "I will save the baba."
Soma is looking so pale
And growing weak, too tired to talk now.
She is almost slipping away
As Ula takes her sharpest flint,
And presses it into Soma's belly.
Startled eyes open wide, fearful,
Then eyes lock with understanding,
As Soma drifts away.

There is no time to waste,
And Ula expertly slices open the belly.
She calls out to Tula for more light
While she carefully makes an incision
Into the womb.
There is blood everywhere now
As she fully opens the womb
To reveal the baba.
She tries to lift the baba out,
But its head seems stuck in the pelvis,
No time to be gentle,
She pulls with all her might.

The baba is silent, but a small heart beats
Although the colour is bluish,
And Ula is not sure if the baba is breathing.
She briskly rubs the little body,
Then holds it upside down by the ankles
And slaps it twice on the back.
There is a faint cry now,
And Ula cuts and ties the cord.
She gently wraps the baba
In a soft deer hide,
And hands the baba to Suta
To rush down and put on Ola's breast.

The hides are soaked in blood
And the cave appears red
Bathed in the blaze of the flames outside.
Tula will never forget the stench, as he looks at
His mada covered in Soma's blood.
Ula is sitting silently beside the lifeless body,
Too much in grief
To even cry or talk.
She can hear the Clan wailing now
As they are told of Soma's death,
She can hear Faru sobbing
As he rushes up to the cave.

Epilogue

I am known as Fasoma and I am one full hands and six full seasons of age. My mada was Soma, always remembered for her courage. She died at my birth and is buried in the birthing cave. I think of her every day, and always remember her in my chants.

My loving fada is Faru, once an Outsider, now a much-loved Clan elder. His thoughts are sometimes confused, but his memories of his early times with the Clan still seem very clear. He does little work now but we all love him and look after him. My loving partner is Tibula, and we shall be having our first baba any moon. How I wish my mada could be here for the birth, but dear Suta will be helping me.

I have fair skin like the Clan, but my body is taller and more slender like the Outsiders. My voice sounds different from the other Clan members', and I am well known for my singing abilities. My fada still likes to do some singing with me. Like all the younger Clan members I can speak the Outsiders' language.

The Clan members often talk about our greater fertility the full season after the Outsiders arrived. Generally Clan couples have just one or two children at the most in their lifetimes, so the three babas coming at the same time was very unusual. Ula has always said that she thinks our low fertility is because of the Clan females' strenuous way of life, with lots of physical activity such as long walks, heavy lifting and constant hunting.

Ula has said how things changed while the Leader lived with the Clan, and the surviving females were not allowed to do their normal work, and had to spend much more time around the cave complex. She thinks this changed our fertility. We accept this explanation, because once life went back to normal for us after the Leader left, then the number of babas was fewer again. Generally most Clan members will die by the time they reach four full hands of full seasons, and again Ula believes this is due to our strenuous way of life.

Tula will always hold a special place in our Clan history. It is chanted that every full season since my birth, Tula would go out alone and mark on his mapa where and when the herd of the Great Hairy Beast had arrived. Six full seasons ago, when the children were grown up enough, Tula took them out for their first hunt. He was particularly excited to be finally going on his first hunt of the Great Hairy Beast, as he had been waiting for so many full seasons. My fada would not join the hunters, as he said it was too dangerous. The animals were so big.

Tula had prepared a special hooded contraption to throw over the head of the Great Hairy Beast, believing that if the animal was temporarily unable to see, then it could be killed more easily. Unfortunately when he threw the contraption over the animal's head, the poor animal was so startled that it stumbled and fell, and rolled on top of him. The Clan stopped the hunt immediately and prodded the frightened animal to move away, only to find that Tula had been crushed to death. The wailing Clan members carried Tula's crushed body back to the cave, where he was buried.

Our grief at that time was overwhelming, as Tula was so loved by us all. Also, there has never been anyone else in the Clan quite like him, so we understand that his contribution to the Clan has been irreplaceable. Tula always said it was after his contact with the Outsiders that he started getting new ideas about how to make different things, such as the mapa and various contraptions to help us capture the animals more easily. Tula used to call these ideas his 'inventions' and I am sure that if he had lived longer there would have been many more of these.

My fada has always said that he thinks that Tula would have had a very good life back in his village, if he had gone back there to live with the Leader. He says that Tula's inventions would have made him very popular and well known with the village people, even more so than with the Clan. Since Tula's death, the Clan has never again hunted the Great Hairy Beast as we realise our numbers are just too small. We cannot take the risk of another death or the serious injury of a Clan member. Also, since Tula's death, sadly no one goes out anymore with the mapa.

Ula, being another irreplaceable Clan member, has managed to find new ways to overcome the shortage of fat, and we have continued with the success of that special bison hunt by Tula, Suta and my fada. We all appreciate and recognise that Ula's courage, unselfish acts and calm manner greatly helped the Clan to survive the brutal encounter with the Outsiders. It must have been a very difficult thing for her, pretending to be the Mother Goddess while the Leader and his Outsiders lived with the Clan. She rarely talks about it now, but I do believe the whole experience stole away some of her inner happiness.

Once I remember hearing her talk about the Outsiders and the Mother Goddess to Tula and my fada. She asked them, "How do you think things might have been different when the Outsiders came, if they did not have their belief in the Mother Goddess?" I was listening very intently, waiting for their reply, but neither Tula nor my fada gave any answer. Perhaps this question was just too hard for them to answer. Such a pity as I certainly thought it was a very good question. I have often thought about this question myself.

Ula has always been like a mada to me, and has always been very loving. But sadly, I can see that Ula has never really recovered from Tula's death, when she seemed to become very tired and old. I fear she will not live much longer. Tibula and I think she is just holding on to see the successful birth of our baba, and after that, hopefully she will be able to die peacefully. I have really enjoyed my talks with Ula and the Clan members this last moon cycle, and now have an even deeper appreciation of Ula's contribution to the Clan.

The Leader has never returned, nor have any other Outsiders come into our land. We know that one day more will come, as my fada explains that his people like to move around and explore more than the Clan members do. We do not really expect future meetings for our Clan, and we can only hope that future meetings for other clans will be more peaceful than our meeting with the Outsiders was. Fada says that will really just depend on the type of person the next Leader will be, as to whether he is a good or a bad person.

I am busy preparing the birthing cave when Tibula calls out for me to quickly come to be with Ula. When I see her I am very upset, for at this moment she seems so still and looks so small. Her eyes are closed and her breathing is very shallow. I think she must be dying. But I am more alarmed, because to me she does not look peaceful. I have noticed that during my pregnancy, Ula has hardly mentioned the coming birth of my baba. But at this very moment, I finally understand why. Suta is holding Ula's hand, and I lean down close to Suta to tell her that I have something very urgent to ask her.

After that I go straight to Ula and take her other hand. I want to cry but dare not, as I want my voice to stay strong and clear. "Ula," I say, desperate to have her hear me. "Ula, can you hear me? Suta has agreed to save the baba if I start to bleed. We will do whatever has to be done to save the baba. Ula, you do not have to worry. Suta understands what to do. Ula, we will save the baba. Ula, can you hear me? I do have my mada's courage!" I think her eyelids may have fluttered, but I am not really sure, as my own eyes are choked with tears.

There are three rasping breaths and then silence. Death and birth are both part of life, and strange how they often they seem to come close together. "*Life brings death, and death can give life,*" I say.

The others repeat, "*Life brings death. Death can give life.*" Then the Clan members start to sob and wail at the Clan's greatest loss ever.

I am still holding Ula's hand, when I whisper in a faltering voice, "Ula, what were you thinking in your last instant?" I can't stop wondering if Ula has heard the words I spoke just before she died. Suddenly I have to draw breath with a sharp pain in my stomach. Now I can feel some warm wetness running down my legs. I am very afraid, but I must look down. Yes if I have to, I will have my mada's courage.

Bibliography

I wish to acknowledge the following books as resource material for my work:

Mellars P. *The Neanderthal Legacy: An Archaeological Perspective from Western Europe*. Princeton: Princeton University Press, 1996.

Oppenheimer S. *Out of Eden: The Peopling of the World*. London: Constable and Robinson, 2003.

Sawyer GJ, Deak V. *The Last Human: A Guide to Twenty-Two Species of Extinct Humans*. New Haven: Yale University Press, 2007.

Schrenk F, Müller S. *The Neanderthals* (English translation). London: Routledge, 2009.

Stringer C, Andrews P. *The Complete World of Human Evolution*. London: Thames and Hudson, 2005.

Tuniz C, Gillespie R, Jones C. *The Bone Readers: Atoms, Genes and the Politics of Australia's Deep Past*. Sydney: Allen & Unwin, 2009.

Thankyou to Helena Newton www.helenanewton.com for her copyediting and proofreading services.

A very special thankyou to my daughter, Dior, for her proofreading assistance, and enthusiastic encouragement of this work.

Glossary

a full season is a year
a moon cycle is a month
half a moon cycle is a fortnight
a moon is a day (i.e. 24 hours)
dark moon means night-time
light moon means daytime
moon time means early evening
mid dark moon means midnight

bata bata means bye-bye
meta meta means thank you

Great Hairy Beast is a mammoth
animal with sharp teeth is a wolf
cave animal with sharp claws is a cave bear
animal with soft eyes is a deer
animal with head bones is a reindeer
animal with long tail is a wild horse
animal that moos is an auroch
animal with fatty neck is a bison

five full hands of full seasons is fifty years
two full hands of full seasons is twenty years
one full hands is ten